CEN DON

Mrs
Hudson's
Diaries

Mrs Hudson's Diaries

A View From the
Landing at 221b

BARRY CRYER
&
BOB CRYER

The Robson Press

First published in Great Britain in 2012 by
The Robson Press (an imprint of Biteback Publishing Ltd)
Westminster Tower
3 Albert Embankment
London SE1 7SP

Internal images on pages 10, 22, 28, 40, 70, 84, 122, 130 and 162 © Getty;
images on pages 48, 102, 150 and 172 © Press Association.

Every reasonable effort has been made to trace copyright holders of
material reproduced in this book, but if any have been inadvertently
overlooked the publishers would be glad to hear from them.

ISBN 978-1-84954-390-3

10 9 8 7 6 5 4 3 2 1

A CIP catalogue record for this book is available from the British Library.

Set in Baskerville
Cover design by Namkwan Cho

Printed and bound in Great Britain by
CPI Group (UK) Ltd, Croydon CR0 4YY

With love to
Terry, Tony, Jayne, Evan, Dave, Jack, Matt, Ruby, Tom,
Archie, Suzannah, Hope, Martha and Connie

Contents

Acknowledgements

To everyone at Biteback Publishing and the Robson Press for helping us find the keys to the kitchen door at 221b.

To Kirsten Wright at Amanda Howard Associates and Sarah Chanin at Roger Hancock Ltd for their invaluable support.

To Lee Jackson's brilliant social history of Victorian London (www.victorianlondon.org) – an obsession generously shared.

To Stephen Moffat and Mark Gatiss for raising the bar.

To everyone at the Save Undershaw Campaign (www.saveundershaw.com) for their monumental efforts to preserve Sir Arthur Conan Doyle's home for the nation.

To Conan Doyle himself, without whom this book would not have been possible.

To Oliver Philpott, without whom this book would have been a very different experience.

Preface

*O*ne frosty winter morning last year, somewhere in the vaults of the bank of Cox & Co. at Charing Cross, we found a battered biscuit tin with the word 'Hudson' painted upon the lid.

Inside, lay the single greatest Holmes-related discovery for nearly a hundred years: the diaries of Sherlock Holmes's landlady, Mrs Hudson. We believe it emphatically completes the Sherlockian jigsaw that is the fragmented canon.

We are now able to pass this gold on to you, dear reader, in the form of these carefully selected entries. Not since Sir Arthur Conan Doyle laid down his pen has there been the same sense of expectation in the publishing world.

Conan Doyle left us only a handful of references and a lot to be desired on the subject of Mrs Hudson. This is an error we are now happy to correct. Everything you've ever needed to know about this remarkable woman can be found between these two covers. And we can also answer the long-running and tantalising mystery of Mrs Hudson's first name: it's Sarah.

For further insights into this incredible discovery, we now leave you in the capable hands of this book's researcher, Oliver Philpott. His footnotes and annotated images represent a veritable treasure trove of hitherto unseen Victorian social history, as witnessed by our worthy landlady. So, handle with care…

Barry Cryer and Bob Cryer
San Marino, 2012

Mrs Hudson's biography
by Oliver Philpott

1840 Born Sarah Richardson in Bermondsey. She is believed to have come from a tanning family, originally from Yorkshire, although early research cannot establish the exact location. Permit me to speculate on it being Haworth, not only home of the Brontës but also to twelve different species of bat.

1853 Mrs Hudson begins her working life as a factory runner in East London.

1860 Aged twenty, she marries the man who would go on to become Victorian London's foremost match entrepreneur. Her betrothal to Arthur Hudson takes place on 13 May at St Vincent's, Langley Road, Clerkenwell, where the pulpit is believed to be the only surviving example of a baroque balustrade.

1862 Early research indicates that Mr Hudson died in a gas explosion, possibly on the 3rd or 4th of April. Only one of his boots was recovered from the scene, apparently with the laces missing. He left Mrs Hudson with sufficient funds to purchase a pair of small rooms in Bow.

1870 Mrs Hudson trades up to a house in Clerkenwell before taking possession of 221b Baker Street, a modest terraced house not far from Gower Street, at the time London's finest example of a French cobble.

1881 The First Boer War begins. By the end of the Second Boer War, the death toll was (approx.) 53,000. Edison invents an early form of steel pressure cooker, killing two assistants in the process. Also, Sherlock Holmes and Dr Watson move in to 221b.

NOTE

Whilst reading these diaries, one may notice the odd brief footnote. These have been crafted by yours truly, Oliver Philpott, for your greater understanding of the period. These are my humble attempts to lead you gently by the hand through the narrow streets of Victorian London; streets that are by turns treacherous and confusing to even the most diligent researcher (modesty forbids!). I hope you enjoy this journey as much as I enjoyed mapping it for you. Tally-ho!

O. P.

Crawley, 2012

Found on top of the diaries:

Claridge's
Brook Street
Mayfair
London, W.
2 November 1914

My dear Watson,

I fear the East wind has finally come but not from Flanders as expected – somewhere much closer to home. I have just returned from a rare visit to Baker Street and now write to you with the gravest of news.

I felt it meet to drop in on our former lodgings whilst I was visiting London from Sussex and I trust you have done the same these last few years. Martha accompanied me and Billy was there to welcome us, you'll be pleased to know. However, rather than his usual cheery greeting, he was in the poorest of spirits. I therefore write these next few lines with a heavy heart.

It pains me to inform you of the death of our worthy landlady.

She died at one minute past eleven on 31 July having fulfilled her duties. There was no mystery surrounding her passing.

I had only missed her by a day but will continue to miss the one and only Mrs H.

I fear that this news will come at a cost which will give you pain, my dear Watson. I didn't get the chance to say goodbye to her but I hope that by some chance you have visited and that this news is tempered by that thought.

Billy told me that there was quite a celebration for her sixty-fourth year and that her stately tread was felt that day as surely as it was the day that we moved in. Little did we know, as we were coming to our country's aid, what revels we were missing. A small service of remembrance has been arranged by Finsbury boxing club in accordance with her wishes. I fear study will prevent me from travelling and I leave our contribution to the attendance of tenants past to you, my dear friend, should the need arise.

Before I left, the most remarkable thing happened as I gave my respects to the mute. Billy, amidst sobs and mumblings, thrust a package into my hands with instructions for it to be passed on to you for safe keeping. Closer inspection revealed the bounty to be a stack of notebooks. It seems our Mrs H. was something of a chronicler, like yourself. By cunning questions and ejaculations of wonder you could always elevate my simple art, which is but systematised common sense, into a prodigy. In your case, I've always maintained that a confederate who foresees your conclusions and course of action is always dangerous, but one to whom each development comes as a perpetual surprise, and to whom the future is always a closed book, is indeed an ideal helpmate. However, it seems little astonished our landlady, and the tomes certainly confirm the very high opinion which I had formed of her abilities as a gossip.

Mycroft has charge of my London affairs and he can point you to their presence in pigeonhole H., done up with a blue ribbon and inscribed 'Hudson'. A copy of the Practical Handbook of Bee Culture, with Some Observations upon the Segregation of the Queen, also awaits Lestrade, as requested.

And for yourself, an occasional weekend visit would be most welcome.

Pray give my greetings to the current Mrs Watson, and believe me to be, my dear fellow,

Very sincerely yours,

Sherlock Holmes

P.S. Come at once if convenient – if inconvenient come all the same.

The very worst tenant in London 1881–90

1881

1 January

Well, here I am writing a diary.

5 January

Martha[1] has informed me that the purpose of writing a diary is that there is not really a purpose at all. She says that I should come back after a year and find that my thoughts will make sense.

Well, what with all the comings and goings at 221b, I wonder whether any of the following will ever make sense?

This morning, the bell rang. Mr Rawlings (known in the Music Halls as the Great Mysto) was in his room practising another one of his 'tricks'. I had to take him the famous 'bucket of sand' that

---

1 Martha Reynolds was the maid at 221b. There were two Reynolds families in Marylebone at that time; one was well known for its religious non-conformity, whereas the other, as far as I can tell, wasn't.

he needs to make an elephant disappear. You have to see it to believe it. And many do.

6 January

A very cold wind. Chestnut Charlie[2] told me that he found his stall halfway up Great Portland Street before he caught up with it. By the time the children had snaffled their share, Charlie said he'd lost half of his stock. Poor man. So I invited him in from the cold. As I write, he's still thawing out by the fire.

7 January

What an odd thing it is to write a diary. Martha keeps a diary and she tells me her auntie does the same. Well, if it's good enough for Mrs Hemple,[3] it's good enough for me! Had to let Mr Rawlings in again as the Great Mysto keeps losing his key. He might be able to magic an elephant from thin air, but ask him where his key is and he's quite lost.

---

2 Chestnut Charlie was just one of many street vendors plying their trade at this time. Others included Oyster Willy and the Cockle Sisters.

3 Your worthy researcher can find no evidence of a Hemple family in Marylebone at the time, whether related to the Reynolds family or not. However, 'to hemple' was perhaps a colloquial expression that conflated the words 'hem' and 'trample' to produce a neologism that is yet to be determined. Rest assured, yours truly is on the case!

8 January

Now, about my resolutions this year. I have one and that is to keep a diary.

1 February

Mr Rawlings on the first floor has informed me that he is to sail for America on Tuesday morning. I asked him if he was taking the elephant with him and he laughed. He's given me two tickets for his farewell performance on Saturday at The Tivoli. What a treat, I do enjoy a night at the music hall.

11 February

New tenants in the first floor rooms. Beds turned down.

A doctor no less! I didn't catch the other gentleman's name. His signature is quite ragged. I think his name is Shylock.

13 February

Seems his name is Sherlock. Not that it matters; it'll be Mr Holmes from now on.

14 February

The doctor seems a most trustworthy gentleman, but his acquaintance, this Mr Holmes, must be the very worst tenant in London. I wouldn't put up with his behaviour, but his payments are so princely. There's his stinking chemistry bench and the jack-knife holes in the mantelpiece, but the worst of it happened this morning.

I was busy kneading a loaf when I heard the most almighty

banging from upstairs. Now, the clouds had gathered and a storm was brewing but it seemed a little early for thunder. Then it started again and I realised it must be coming from the first floor. So, up I went and knocked on the door. Another volley of banging. I went in and found the whole room fogged up with smoke. My new tenant, Mr Holmes, was sat there in his armchair firing a gun. I think I must have been too shocked to be angry. Then I looked at my poor wall. There, in perfectly straight lines, were the letters 'V. R'. I looked at Mr Holmes for an explanation. Instead, he carried on looking at the letters and fired a final full stop after the 'R'. Now I'm as much a patriot as the next landlady, but how is this sort of behaviour going to pay the rent?

Well, he assures me that he is going to be practising his detection on my premises. Seems to me he spends more time practising his violin,[4] so I'll just have to take his word for it that he has an occupation. I wouldn't mind about the violin only it jangles my nerves! And to think, Dr Watson says he plays most delightfully.

I said to the doctor, about his bull terrier James and the situation with our cat, Mr Disraeli, that he might have to put the dog down, menace that he is. He said to me 'I'm a doctor, not a vet!' I couldn't

---

4   A Stradivarius (not an Amati!), which is a type of Cremona violin, worth five hundred guineas. He purchased it in Tottenham Court Road for fifty-five shillings. In today's money, that would be £165, enough to pay Mr Wayne Rooney to play football for sixteen minutes!

argue with him there and, before I knew it, he'd helped me carry the ash bucket to the back door. He won't get round me that way! Well, maybe a little.

Will any good come of this tenancy? Well, as I sit here at the kitchen table, with Martha knitting at my elbow, I am happy to say that as long as they pay their rent on time, I couldn't give a fig.

4 March

He's back again. Mr Holmes's visitor. That's the third time this week and today he had to sit in my kitchen because they had someone else up there. Never gives his name but Mr Holmes agrees to see him all the same. Funny little mouse he is. Barely said a word, just sat there rubbing his hands. I offered him a cup of tea but no sooner had the kettle boiled, the bell rang, and he scurried upstairs.

5 March

His name is Lestrade[5] and he's a well-known detective. At least that's what he told me. I asked him if he was here to arrest Mr Holmes and he laughed. Much activity upstairs. The dog's gone though. Mr Disraeli will be pleased.

---

5 According to Dr Watson's case notes, Inspector Lestrade's first name began with a G. As his surname suggests French heritage, may I suggest 'Gaston'?

6 March

What did I say? No visitors without my say so. First it's that policeman from down the road and now it's half a dozen street arabs treating my place like it was their own. They were ringing my bell more than once, when I've only just had it polished. Any more of this and they'll be chased off, the lot of them.

And lamb's up a penny.

7 March

Street organ came again today. Can't join in due to my calves but try and hold Martha back. Sat for a good hour watching events. Even the census man joined in, halfway between asking my occupation and my age. I told him I'm as old as my tongue and a little older than my teeth. And he said, 'Well which is it?' The larrikin.

8 March

It's been twenty years since I heard the name of Madame Charpentier.[6] We had another Inspector visiting Mr Holmes this morning – the third this week – called Gregs[7] or something I think he was, and I heard him clearly mentioning her name. Even though she was a solid gold troublemaker back when I lived in Clerkenwell, to have your son bundled away and your daughter leered at, well, I

---

6   I think you'll find it was twenty-one years.

7   Inspector Tobias Gregson of Scotland Yard. No mysterious first initial here, thank goodness!

wouldn't wish that on anyone. It reminds me of the old days when my Arthur[8] was still with us. Bless you dear man, wherever you may be.

12 April

Dear Arthur,

I can't believe it's been twenty years, my little Prince. Well, where does the time go? Just today, I was hanging out some washing in the back when I heard a bird chirruping away and I thought it was you. It sounded like the whistle you used to do when you came home. I thought I was back in Clerkenwell. I half expected to hear your dear footsteps skipping in the hall. 'We toasted you, my Queen!' you used to say. And I'd say 'And how many more did you toast?'

19 April

Here's a strange thing that happened. Martha found a little kitten in the back yard this morning and we have decided to take him in. The poor mite is still a little unsure of the kitchen but when I fed him some smoked mackerel he cheered up. In fact, so much so, that when Mr Disraeli[9] attempted to take some for himself, the little one gave him a punch on his nose. Then, would you believe it, Mrs Turner came in with such a sad expression and told us that the real

---

8   The aforementioned (late) Mr Hudson. He of the missing boot.

9   The cat, as you will recall from the bull terrier episode.

Mr Disraeli, Lord Beaconsfield,[10] *had died. The house has been in a hush since. I have decided to call the kitten O'Connell*[11] *as a tribute to the late Earl.*

---

10 Benjamin Disraeli was the Prime Minister of Great Britain and Ireland from 27 February 1868 until 1 December 1868 and 20 February 1874 until 21 April 1880 (as you know!). His great rival William Ewart Gladstone was so overcome during the eulogy to the Commons that he got diarrhoea.

11 This is a reference to a famous exchange in the Commons that Disraeli had with the Irish MP Daniel O'Connell. O'Connell called Disraeli a fanatical slave and Disraeli called O'Connell a cave dweller (nothing changes!). I think Mrs Hudson is making a satirical joke here.

Philpott's photo corner

The photographs within this book were found in Mrs Hudson's diaries, along with the letters and recipes also contained here.

Unfortunately, only two bear annotation and confirm their connection to our worthy landlady. Therefore one can only speculate as to whether the others belonged to Mrs Hudson at all. Nevertheless, they undoubtedly deserve inclusion, painting as they do a comprehensive portrait of life in Baker Street and the surrounding area.

I don't mind confessing that I found this lack of specific detail quite irksome. However, dear reader, we soldier on and I will endeavour to provide you with as much background as possible.

Onward and upward!

This appears to be a picture of 'The Great Bilbo' and his dancing bear 'Bruin', who were well known on the streets of London at the time.[12] The Great Bilbo and Bruin once featured in the finale of the Royal Command performance of 1912 at the Palace Theatre. Records show that following that performance, Bruin, fuelled by champagne, escaped The Great Bilbo and roamed the streets of Soho. He even escaped being apprehended by the police and a veterinary surgeon. At one point, it was said that he entered a workman's café and was served with a loaf of bread. Tragically, Bruin died shortly afterwards, whilst dancing enthusiastically for an assembled throng on the Embankment. His body fell into the Thames, and The Great Bilbo, who had caught up with him just before, was dragged in with him. Fortunately, The Great Bilbo managed to swim to safety but Bruin was last seen floating towards Kent. Rumour has it that his body was recovered by some fishermen and that he was stuffed for exhibition, but I have, as yet, been unable to verify this.

---

12 This picture should be entitled 'Bear With Me'!

1882

14 August

A blazing hot day today with little chance of anyone moving. Hannah and I sat in the coolest part of the scullery and talked of nothing but the 'Melancholy Event' in her street. Ann, an old lady who never came out of her house, died on the twelfth of consumption. She had nearly been the wife of Mr Oliver Neid, who we all knew from Tottenham Court Road and was something of a cad. She had also been a former mistress of Hannah's, when she was a maid, whose service she left owing to a misunderstanding. Ann called her a fool and Hannah made the same answer back. The old woman never forgave her. Hannah was very sad but cheered up when I told her of the story of the two human ears that were mailed in a cardboard box to a woman in Croydon.

17 September

The butcher boy was meant to call last Monday with some offal. What greeted me at the back door was no boy. He was a gentleman, probably in his thirties, and he said I should remember him.

I confessed that I didn't. Then I asked him what he'd done with the butcher boy. He said don't look at the offal too closely in case you find an apron. What a wicked thing to say, I said. Then he grinned an unmistakable grin and I went quite pale. It's been over twenty years since we both earned 5s a week shunting glass around that factory in Bow. It was D. L.

The first thing to note was that he seemed rather taken aback by my situation and kept offering to doff his cap to me as 'Mistress of the House'. How you'd have laughed, Arthur, to see me and D. L. pretending to be Queen and servant.

The years have not been kind to him. I did not want to upset the poor man by prying but it seems that Molly at the factory may have led him a merry dance once upon a time and broken his heart. And all those years near the furnace have left him capable of little but running meat around to the likes of me. I wish there was something I could do to help him, but he assures me that Mr Yarrow is kind to him and he's just happy to play his part.

He promised to bring me sweetmeats tomorrow. I must confess I blushed and went a bit giddy. I've forgotten what they tasted like. Well, I was unsure at first and then I thought, 'I don't care what people say' and then I thought 'Yes, I do', and I declined. I feel silly now.

18 September

I was talking to Mrs Turner today and given it was a Monday, thoughts turned to bluing.[13] *She's had terrible problems with her*

---

13 'Bluing' is a reference to the practice of creating a colloidal suspension in water in order to promote whiteness in dirty linen. An early example of a 'blue rinse', perhaps?

maid, Kate, putting too much oxalic in the wash. I don't want to sound smug, but Martha uses Sawyer's and we never have that problem. Mrs T. is forever complaining about Sawyer's Crystal Blue but I'm sure she'll stop now. In fact Hannah Brayley often says that Mrs T. complains until she is 'bluine' the face! Mrs T. thinks Hannah ever so silly. She also mentioned that Mr Yarrow had a new 'boy'. I pretended not to know. No sweetmeats.

2 November

Inspector Lestrade popped in again today for a cup of tea and a chat. The more I see of him, the more he interests me. He obviously respects Mr Holmes and they're always having their long chats, but afterwards, 'old Moaner' as I call him, seems not very happy. He goes on about Mr Holmes telling him his job and it makes him cross but I know that these chats are important to him. Moaner goes away and remembers something Mr Holmes has said and that gives him the idea of what to do. I'm sure Mr Holmes doesn't take any credit but he doesn't need to, does he? But, oh dear, the Inspector does go on as if he's not getting credit. I said this to him one day and, mercy, that started him off. It reminded me of the boy at my Arthur's school who was smarter than the others, but all the other boys could do was find fault with him. There was another time when the Inspector came in here full of himself and on top of the world. He'd just solved a case and couldn't wait to tell me about it. Funny thing is, I remember that case and how Mr Holmes had shouted down the stairs to Moaner, 'I think you'll find the answer is in the bank vault!' So when he comes in here bragging about a case, I now realise it's usually Mr Holmes who's put his finger on the solution. I'm beginning to think he might be quite an intriguing tenant.

As the reader will know, Holmes's image, in the absence of any photographs (which is in itself a mystery) has become iconic: the deerstalker hat and the calabash pipe, depicted by artists in order to attempt to get to the heart of the appearance of the man. If he did indeed sport these immediately recognisable 'props', whence came the reason? Something was nagging at my brain – a picture I came across in previous research for a book I was writing on the subject of Russian folk singers in the nineteenth century.[14] This particular portrait depicted Yuri Gerschenko (1820–94), a popular balladeer in his day, whose distinctive look riveted me. He wore a hat that can only be described as a deerstalker and cradled a pipe indistinguishable from that apparently owned by Holmes (although I believe the Meerschaum/Calabash community is split over this one). Further research unearthed the fact that he was a policeman, who sang at community gatherings in the evenings. The constant coincidences occurring in my investigative work in the service of this book (compare the assassination of Lord Crumbrooke later) led me to think that there is a positive undercurrent of synchronicity beneath the whole Holmes canon. There had even been an Inspector Holmes in the City of London police force only years before. One can only speculate (along with Hamlet) that there are more things in heaven and earth, Horatio, than are dreamt of in your philosophy. I venture to suggest that I could not have put it better myself.

---

14 *Balalaikas and Samovars: Songs from The Steppes* (Rushton Press, 1985).

1883

22 March

D. L. again today. I have to say I am getting quite used to his visits. On a few occasions, when Mr H. is upstairs practising his violin, D. L. has been in the kitchen. D. L. likes to pretend that the sound of the violin is a fly buzzing around. He chases it to the back door and ushers it out. D. L. says it works very well with Mendelssohn but less so with Smetana as the fly can be a little sluggish. I cannot tell the difference myself, but I do find it funny.

28 March

I was sitting in Langbourn's Coffee House on Lombard Street earlier when I overheard two cabbies talking about their wives. Such language. I am pleased that I walk everywhere.

7 September

I'm sat here with Mr Disraeli. What a naughty boy. He went missing the other day.

I wasn't worried at first but then I started asking around and Hannah said she'd seen him in the alley, so, I went and there he was. I called him, but as we all know, you can't call a cat – they never come. Dogs do but cats seem to have a mind of their own. I called and called but he ran off again. What possessed me, I don't know, but I happened to mention it to Mr Holmes this morning, whilst he was sitting in his chair, smoking away. By the way, when he's puffing on his pipe, I feel like I'm walking into a fog but that's neither here nor there (as the man said when he put his truss on upside-down – lawks! – that must be a rude joke Hannah Brayley told me). Anyway, when I told him, Mr Holmes sprang up straight away and said 'Mr Disraeli is in Courtney Road, third elm tree along with the withered limb, directly opposite the fire station.' How on earth did he know that, I thought? Whatever it is he does, he's obviously very good at it. Sure enough, when Mr Holmes and I went to look, there was Mr Disraeli up that very tree, bold as brass, licking himself. He started mewing (Mr Holmes, not the cat). And that cheeky Mr Disraeli looked and looked, and then jumped into Mr Holmes's arms. I wanted to clap, so help me. 'There we are Mrs Hudson!' said Mr Holmes. 'The prodigal returns.' What a day that was! I couldn't believe it. I've a mind to tell Dr Watson about what happened today. He could call it 'Sherlock Holmes and the case of the cat up a tree'. Anyway, I gave the great man extra biscuits with his claret on the strength of it.

17 September

Just yesterday, I was standing in Baker Street talking to Mrs Turner when I see Mrs Brayley gazing up at the rooftops and pointing. A crowd soon gathered and she continued pointing. After a few moments, she walked away, leaving the crowd baffled. Mrs Turner seemed baffled as well. Hannah does make me laugh.

I find the wallpaper in this picture very interesting. After some research, I learned that the wallpaper is not typical of its time, in terms of thickness and general layout. Why would this be? My only theory is that it may be the work of foreign decorators (who worked in a different pattern) but whence came the columns? I will obviously endeavour to pursue this line of enquiry, but not, alas, in time for the publication of this book. As regards the couple in front of the wall, they may be family, neighbours or not connected in any way to Mrs Hudson. The man's collar is interesting, insofar as the 'wing' was rarely worn with a single-breasted jacket (depicted). I glean this fascinating sliver of information in Garth Winslow's *Neck & Neck: The History of the Collar 1642–1945.*[15]

---

15 Gerund Press, 1992. I've noticed one or two errors in this book, but space does not permit expanding on them here.

1884

4 March

Inspector Lestrade popped into the kitchen for a cup of tea again after he'd seen Mr H.

I like him, but he still spends too much of his time here complaining about people claiming credit for something he's done. I think that's a bit rich when I know for a fact Mr H. has often let him take the credit for things that Mr H. has done. Still, never mind, it all comes out in the wash as my mother used to say.

The other day, Inspector Gregson, who Mr Lestrade thinks is a bit of a dandy, stopped by and was talking about a case they were working on. He's as bad as Moaner – talk about little boys fighting under a blanket, I had to calm him down. If these men continue to behave as if they're in their club, then I will have to start charging for their tea.

5 April

I'm sitting here chuckling whilst I should be polishing my brass salvers. I don't mind telling you that he's done it again.

Yesterday, I was having two stair rods replaced (for the third time this year). They had been broken by Mr H.'s heels of course, who goes up and down those stairs several times a day. I am always complaining about it to him but when I mentioned it this time one of the workmen piped up in his defence. How he knew so much about Mr H. was beyond me, but there he was, bold as brass, telling me that Mr Holmes was obviously an exceptional case. Well, I had no idea what he was on about, so I asked the gentleman to explain himself. Without a pause, he points at his heels and says 'Behold! The curse!' Well, I didn't understand what that meant and I was ready to dismiss him, when he winks at me and rips his moustache off. I nearly fainted on the spot. It was Mr Holmes himself. I've never had a tenant like him.

31 September

Today, I saw a crowd around Hannah Brayley, who was talking into the slot of a pillar box. She said 'How long have you been in there?' and do you know what, I think they all thought there really was someone in there. She carried on asking questions and then walked away, leaving some of the crowd talking to the box. She should go on the stage, that one. I'd pay to see her.

1 November

The rain fell all day and Martha has a leak in her room. Poor thing spent last night with her umbrella up. I must have the tiles looked at this week.

Another enigma! I could ascertain no direct connection with Mrs Hudson in this picture, but the woman's collar, complete with medallion, set me on the chase. Close examination with my trusty magnifying glass[16] revealed a small trowel thereon. Trowel/brick-layer/mason, perhaps? Come with me now as we travel down a Masonic road. Women were not members of the order, so why was a woman wearing it? The picture does not reveal a wedding ring or an absence thereof, so I cannot conjecture as to whether she was wearing it as an unspoken tribute to her husband. I can only assume she did not recognise the significance of the trowel and wore it unwittingly. The Freemasons operated then (as now, apparently) under a veil of secrecy and this picture unequivocally perpetuates that! A thought occurs. Is this perhaps a Mason in female attire? The plot thickens![17]

---

16 Move over Mr Holmes!

17 I venture Holmes himself would relish this conundrum. 'The Strange Affair of the Trowel Medallion' certainly has a ring to it. A three-pipe problem indeed.

1885

3 April

D. L. delivered the bacon and I was a little shocked by the price. So much so, I think I was a little short with him. Mr Yarrow likes to add a penny every spring it seems but tuppence[18] this year was uncalled for. D. L. asked me if I would like to go with him to Hyde Park on May Day to see the Chimney Sweep parade[19] on account of his cousin being in the party, but I quickly declined. What if there is a fire? I cannot leave the house if all the chimney sweeps in London are in Hyde Park. The May Day parade is all a little too chaotic for my liking. I think I will save that jaunt for another year. Besides, there's Mr H.'s supper to cook. As Arthur used to say, 'You can't catch all the trains.'

---

18 Tuppence is worth 50p in today's money.

19 In 1893, this parade's monopoly on Hyde Park was challenged by the inaugural 'Muffin Seller's March'. A skirmish ensued by The Serpentine and the police were called. Thirty-eight sweeps and twenty-two muffin sellers were detained. There were no fatalities.

PIG'S LIVER

Cut the liver in half, as a butterfly, taking care to keep it intact. Put in a tin with seasoning of salt and pepper and cover with butter. Leave aside for twenty minutes. Take some chopped bacon, onion and parsley and push inside the liver before tying up with string. Put in a bigger dish with a big piece of bacon wrapped around it, cover it and set in medium oven. Serve it in its own juice with either mustard or some vinegar.

Letter from the Prince of Wales.

London, 11 July 1885

His Royal Highness the Prince of Wales wishes me to inform you, Mr Holmes, that he will be at the villa on the 23rd.[20]

Yours sincerely,

Captain H. Stephenson, R.N., C.B. (Extra Equerry to the Prince of Wales)

---

20 This is obviously a reference to a notorious scandal of the time, over which we will draw a veil.*

*What am I paying you for? – Publisher

1886

27 January

Chestnut Charlie has gone. Wiggins told me that he's found a new life helping out in a Chinese mission house. You never know with some people. Where will our chestnuts come from now?

17 June

Today, Hannah told me Mme Charpentier has these 'spiritual evenings'. She claims to put people in touch with the dead and often speaks with their voice. Well, I told Hannah that I've often wondered what Arthur is up to these days. 'Now's your chance to find out,' she said. I wonder if there is anything in these 'séances'. I'll soon find out as Hannah has already made an appointment.

19 June

Bought a new hat today. Peterson's recommended an ivory spring but I decided to purchase a French bonnet instead. I like the tall crown and the wide brim but Hannah says that I look like a bookie.

21 June

To Camberwell and Mme Charpentier's spiritual evening with Mrs Brayley. On the way there, when I told Hannah to behave herself she just winked at me.

I have to say Mme Charpentier has done rather well for herself. She now lives in the big house at the end of the road – the one she'd always had her eye on. After everything that happened to that poor woman I can't deny that she perhaps deserves a little good fortune. Indeed it was nice to see Alice serving the drinks. Madame is indeed looking older, as you would expect, but there is something of the made-up doyenne about her which is not entirely out of character. When the séance began, we were five in number, including a Mr and Mrs Glossop, who were there to find out the whereabouts of some silver, and another gentleman. Madame began by suddenly addressing the man in a deep baritone voice, which made him cry for some reason and leave the room. We never did catch his name.

She then turned to me and said that my husband wanted to speak with me. Well, I can tell you that sent a shiver down my spine. And then, in the same deep baritone voice, Mme Charpentier says:

'*This is your husband speaking.*'

'*Is that you, Arthur?*' I said.

'*Yes, that's right.*'

'*It doesn't sound much like you.*'

'*I have a bit of a cold, my dear.*'

I was trying to concentrate but Hannah was making this funny snorting sound and kicking my foot under the table.

'*Don't worry my dear, all is well where I am,*' said Mme Charpentier (*in a slightly higher voice this time*).

'*Your cold's cleared up,*' says Hannah and I had to bite my lip.

'*Never mind all that. It's just wonderful to speak to you, my dear.*'

Hannah beamed at Mme Charpentier.

'*Address your dear wife by her name, Arthur!*' she says.

'*Do you mean my pet name for you, my dear?*'

'*No,*' Hannah and I both chimed in.

And then Mme Charpentier started rocking in her chair and moaning.

'*I'm losing him, I'm losing him,*' she wailed.

'*You never found him,*' said Hannah.

'*What was that you said about some silver?*' Mme Charpentier said to the Glossops, in a French accent, for some reason.

Well, that was enough for us, as Hannah was bent double with laughter. I had to escort her out of the room. As we left, I noticed she had put something in the bowl by the door marked 'donations'. I asked her if she thought I should contribute too. '*Don't worry,*' *she said* '*I put a button in for you as well.*'

What an evening. We laughed all the way home doing funny deep voices.

I think that might be the last time I see Mme Charpentier,[21] but then, as a medium, she probably knows that already.

---

21 The account of Mme Charpentier's séance led me to research the shadowy, bizarre world of Victorian mediums (or should that be media?). One account I stumbled on in my diligent research on your behalf (self-praise is no recommendation, I hear you cry!) led me to the story of Lord Crumbrooke. He was not a bona fide member of the nobility as the title was self-bestowed. The dubious 'Lord' became celebrated for his séances, which were on a much more pretentious scale than Mme Charpentier's. He claimed to be able to put people in touch with not only their own deceased family members but figures of international fame and notoriety. He would make the modest claim that the assembled company, sitting with hands joined in the murky ambience of his sitting room in Tulse Hill, would be able to speak to such personalities as Napoleon, Marie Antoinette, King George III and many more. His evocation of Marie Antoinette was not entirely convincing as, at his séances, she appeared to have a north London accent. Even when finally discredited, people would still flock to see his stage show, leading him to 'come out' (in modern parlance) and tour the music halls as a genuine impersonator. He was tragically shot whilst presenting his depiction of Abraham Lincoln. The name of his assassin was Oswald Lee, which, I am sure you will realise, has an uncanny resonance with the tragic events of Dallas in 1963.

CALLING CARDS

Mrs Hudson kept many of the calling cards that passed onto her famous brass salver. Here are just a few that have survived:

Sir Henry Baskerville
Dr J. Mortimer
Sgr Ingnatius Paloma
Mons. Vertus Pugilum
Miss I. Adler
Parson Nicholas
Lady Carrington
J. V. Wilson
Miss V. Hunter
Count Von Kramm
Prof. Summerlee
Lord Cantlemere
Prof. A. M. Toirry
Dr A. C. Smith
Lady Sigerson

This picture is particularly interesting as Mrs Hudson herself has written on the back, 'I've no idea who this is.' Well, that is akin to a red rag put in front of a bull for yours truly. So, plunging into uniform research, I discovered that our be-helmeted candidate was in fact none other than an armed policeman, a member of the special branch who specialised in combating violent crime. His helmet badge denoted membership of 'The Crusaders', as they were known. His belt is interesting. It is, in fact, not the standard issue belt of The Crusaders! Their emblem features a rampant St George sitting atop a Turks head but no sign of that here. In what can only be described as a bout of individualism on the part of our young constable, he is seen sporting a segmented pewter rope twist, typical of the Finchley cadets of the day. We must admire him for that. I confess, I've not been able to detect the source of the belt. The watch chain is self-explanatory and we need not dwell on it here. The window sill is interesting, revealing a briefcase, but the relevance is lost here, my friends. As his boots are rather nondescript, I am unable to muse upon them. All in all, a fairly interesting, if not productive picture, well worthy of inclusion even if only on the grounds of obscurity. His name is unknown, but a colleague here thinks he looks Scottish!

1887

1 March

I visited Mr Yarrow the butcher today and asked after D. L. Mr Yarrow said he hasn't seen him for a month but Mrs Turner came in and mentioned seeing D. L. with a red-headed lady. It seems Molly Rifkind and he have renewed their acquaintance and D. L. has gone to help her run a post office in Somerset. I hope they will be very happy together. It is rather strange that he should agree to take on postal deliveries when he used to complain about all the walking he did for Mr Yarrow, but there you are. If I remember rightly, it was always Molly's skill to get a man to change his mind. I just hope the country air suits him. I'm sure it shall.

20 July

Last evening, I gave Mr H. and the doctor a treat, one I haven't cooked for a long while: my famous boiled tripe.

I cut the tripe up into pieces the size of two inches square and put them into a saucepan containing skim milk, or milk and water if you prefer (I always like to ask the milk boy to deliver my milk and water in separate cans! – makes him chuckle). There should be enough milk to swim the tripe. Then I add some peeled onions, pepper and salt, and a sprig of thyme, and boil gently for at least an hour. When the tripe is done, I get Mr H. and Dr W. to eat it with mustard and well-boiled potatoes. They seemed most impressed, given the groans of delight that came from their room last night. I notice they have yet to rise today but I believe that's because they have been busy working on a case all day. There was certainly plentiful activity on the staircase – all that pacing was probably on account of the fact we had the Prime Minister[22] himself visiting yesterday.

I offered him some tripe but he said no. I wouldn't vote for him even if I could.

4 September

Lestrade and Gregson at it all morning. Gregson was pointing his stubby little sausage fingers at Moaner and I could tell he didn't like it one bit. I've had enough of sitting in the middle of it all. I told them they were behaving like a bunch of little boys, when, would you believe it, a real bunch of little boys came scampering through my kitchen and up the stairs. It was Wiggins and

---

22 Lord Salisbury, I presume.

his urchins[23] *(scraping my wallpaper again) and this time, there seemed to be twice as many of them. I've spoken to Mr H. on more than one occasion about this and you'd think he'd have done something. Well, finally, and with a little grace, he did. Once the noise had stopped and my patience had returned, I was able to get back to Fingers and Moaner. Well I would have if they hadn't left whilst I was upstairs. I give up some days. Feels more like Buffalo Bill's rodeo in here than a lodgings.*

5 September

Dr Watson came in this evening in high spirits. Mr Holmes, however, well, I shouldn't say this, but I am afraid for his health. When the doctor was away he walked and he walked, up and down, and up and down, until I was weary of the sound of his footsteps. Then I heard him talking to himself and muttering, and every time the bell rang he came to the stair head. I hope he's not going to be ill. I tried to say something to him about fetching him some medicine, but he turned on me with such a look. So I decided to have a word with the doctor about things but I may have got it wrong. He gave me cause not to worry, explaining that Mr Holmes has some small matter upon his mind which makes him restless. I

---

23 Mrs Hudson is referring to The Baker Street Irregulars, a gang of impoverished urban children that often helped Sherlock Holmes with his cases in return for a small fee. One can only applaud their enterprise and hope that our own 'youth' of today would take note of this. Only the other day, I had my double-locked town and country bike stolen from outside the library. Apparently, nobody saw it happen and this was at two o'clock in the afternoon. I asked behind the desk but all I got from the staff was a form to fill in and barely anything resembling sympathy. I ask you, what is the world coming to!

told him that I'm used to finding cigars in the coal scuttle but I then mentioned the morocco case I found on the mantle with the syringe in it. I could tell Dr Watson didn't approve of my curiosity, but he suggested that Mr H.'s mind needs such things. Still, it can't be good for him. As the doctor himself said, 'Surely the game is not worth the candle?'

The moon is especially bright tonight and I think we may have a frost in the morning. Time to turn in.

2 December

Well, it's been never a dull moment lately, I can tell you. I was in the kitchen trying to mind my own business when I heard sounds from upstairs. When I say sounds – there was a row going on. I couldn't believe it, Mr Holmes and Dr Watson were at it hammer and tongs. I didn't hear all of it I confess, but when I went to the top of the stairs (doing a bit of light dusting, of course) I did catch some of it. Although I couldn't hear everything the doctor said (he must have been by the window) I wrote most of it down. A little sketch, you could say. And here it is:

'You are my Boswell now, I suppose,' said Mr Holmes, as cross as anything.

'Oh for heaven's sake, Holmes,' said the doctor and then said something about reporting things that happened.

'Why did you have to take my notes and read them?' said Mr H. 'Curiosity killed the cat, dear doctor and it hasn't done my constitution any good.'

Dr Watson replied, but I couldn't hear properly.

Mr H. continued, 'Report the facts, yes, but your purple prose would've made Oscar Wilde blush.'

They started moving about and I remembered I had something on the boil. I missed what happened next but, from the hall, I heard the door slam. It was all I could do to bob back in the kitchen when Dr Watson came clumping down the stairs and out of the front door. I admit it is none of my business, but it is interesting. As Mr Holmes said 'Curiosity killed the cat', and the funny thing was, as Dr Watson left, he nearly shut the door on Mr Disraeli's tail.

Ah! Now we are talking (or rather, looking!). These ladies are the formidable Molloy Sisters, well-known athletes and free-style wrestlers, who toured the country in a show entitled *Amazons Ahoy!*, which featured acrobatics, posing and, of course, wrestling.[24] Each night,[25] the sisters would invite two members of the audience, male or female (or both), to come onto the stage to wrestle with them. Molly (on the left), known as 'The Sioux Slayer', used to dress in Red Indian[26] garb and wield a tomahawk.[27] Dorothy (on the right, holding the book), appeared as 'Battling Boudicca' in a toga and leggings, though not brandishing the umbrella, I fancy. One particular story, related by the esteemed popular entertainment historian Edgar Lofthouse, concerned the fact that, in order to drum up business in the town in which they were appearing, they would announce on the Friday night that the sisters would eat a member of the audience alive on stage. There was always some willing volunteer, infused with alcoholic refreshment and with his pay packet on his person, who would offer himself up for sacrifice. The band would play suitably dramatic music as the sisters laid him on an operating table and proceeded to brandish scalpels, knives and even, on one occasion, a hacksaw. If his nerve had not evaporated by this stage, they would then remove his jacket and roll up his sleeves. One sister would then advance on him with a scalpel/knife/hacksaw held aloft. If the gentleman was still resolved, the other sister would then brush her teeth. Pause. And if there were still signs of compliance, sprinkle pepper and salt on his arm. This usually did the trick, although on occasions she (often Molly) would have to sink her teeth into his arm to yield the required surrender. What halcyon days of entertainment![28]

---

24 There was a third sister, Wendy, but little is known about her history. All we do know is that she preferred not to perform due to her fear of lime.

25 As recounted in Edgar Lofthouse's seminal *History of the Halls*, pp. 145–7 (Corduroy Press, 1987).

26 Pardon me! Native American or First Nation!

27 Made of balsawood, if you'd credit it.

28 The sisters never married.

1888

6 January

Mr dearest Arthur. I greet you and the new year with good news and a coincidence. I have put my rents up again. 6d[29] now means that I can give in to Martha's request for help on the upper floors. No sooner had this happened, than D. L. visited today with something of a surprise request. It seems his nephew, Billy, is in need of some favour, having only just been rescued from the workhouse infirmary. Then, this ten-year-old boy stuck his head out from inside D. L.'s coat and introduced himself as Billy. He is ever so young but ever so eager to please. D. L. told him I liked the Music Hall and, quick as a flash, the young lad started singing a Sydney Fisher song. You know the one about the horse race and the monkey? Well, my heart melted and I hired him immediately. I think it must be because he reminds me of you, my dear. So full of life and good cheer. Martha

---

29 £6.60 in today's money. Probably wouldn't buy you a latte in Baker Street these days.

is already very taken with him. I wanted to introduce Billy to our tenants on the first floor but was politely reminded by the great detective not to disturb him on his birthday.[30] *There were no cards this morning, which I thought was rather sad. So, instead, I got Billy to take a card up from me and, do you know what? He was let in. I think even Mr H. took something of a shine to the lad and he invited him and D. L. to tour the rooms. Unfortunately, Mr H. was cooking up some experiments in his room and there was so much smoke coming from one bottle we had to leave. What will the poor lad think? D. L. said the last time he smelt such a thing he was taking a pipe with a carpet seller from Portland Place.*

7 January

I had the strangest dream last night that Billy was a puppy and we were walking on Exmoor. Somehow I knew where I was going but Billy did not and I had to keep pulling his lead to the top of a hill. A little further on and a man in a hat appeared and began pointing frantically at a town below. 'I am from Porlock,' he said, 'and you won't recognise me until it's too late!' Well, he took his hat off and I'll be blowed if it wasn't you, Arthur. I was awoken by Mr Disraeli clawing at the curtains on the landing and the sound of Billy running to get the first postal delivery. I told Hannah about my dream at tea and she asked me what was in my nightcap. Mr H. and the doctor have gone to Sussex.

---

30 Apparently Holmes's birthday coincided with the Feast of The Epiphany. Make of that what you will.

24 February

Mr H. returned from the doctor's wedding late this evening a little sullen. I asked if he would like some supper but he declined. Poor soul, he does seem a little lost. Mrs B. joked that he may struggle to pay the rent now the doctor has gone. I don't think so.

19 March

I decided that today was the day to see what all the fuss is about. Yes, Billy and I went on the underground railway for the very first time. After visiting Billy's mother we went from Bishop's Road to Farringdon Street.[31] Only four miles, but I can now say it was the longest four miles I ever remember. Very hot, with sulphur, coal dust and horrid fumes from an oil lamp. What a stink! I put my handkerchief over my face, when, would you believe it, the gentleman opposite takes out his pipe and begins puffing away.

By the time we reached Farringdon, I was practically out of breath and near burnt by the heat. Billy was delighted. They say the underground is coming to Baker Street very soon. What is the world coming to? Imagine the noise under your feet. You should have seen Mrs Turner's face when I told her. White as a sheet.

---

31 Quite what Mrs Hudson had been doing for the previous eighteen years, one cannot say, but this particular branch of London's seminal underground railway system had been operational since 1865.

20 March

I was in terrible pain today on account of yesterday's day out. I could hardly breathe in without needing to sit down. The thought of facing those seventeen steps to the first floor is not very appealing. Mr H. has been very quiet of late but today he has been pacing the floor nonstop since this morning's post. I fear I may be needed more. God bless Mrs Turner, who has agreed to help look after things on the upper levels from tomorrow.

The good doctor paid us a visit this evening. How delightful to see him looking so fit and healthy, if a little vague. I was going to ask him about my cough but he seemed distracted. Marriage is the making of most men and I'm sure it will be for Dr Watson. Although, I think you were the making of me, Arthur.

The doctor's visit usually means that something is about to happen. Sure enough, a large gentleman describing himself as Count Von Kramm came sweeping through the hallway, past Billy and Martha and up the stairs. He was all furry collars, silver buttons and waxed hair. Very vulgar. When he left, Mr Holmes looked very pleased indeed. I took this as an opportunity to enquire after the rent but was assured by Dr Watson that it would not be a problem. I think my cough is going.

21 March

The doctor returned at three and he quickly became caught up in his friend's thoughts. He was certainly rather curt with me again today. I wasn't upset as I know it means they are once more working together, just like old times. I cannot say I know Mrs Watson very well, save for her visit last year, but I hope she realises they are like hounds on a scent, those two, when they are at a case.

22 March

Feeling better today. Gave myself the challenge of making breakfast for Mr H. and the doctor. I had no sooner taken them their toast and coffee this morning, when the same gentleman from the other day, dressed in his ridiculous cape and astrakhan fuzz, comes bounding up to the room. Mrs Turner said that the man in question was actually a king. To be honest, I've seen so many different people come through these doors in the last seven years, I wouldn't be the least bit surprised if he was the Queen of Sheba. It wasn't long before all three gentlemen were out in the street boarding a rather impressive looking carriage. As they left, they mentioned a pair of women called Adler and Norton, and it is the first time I've heard Mr H. talk so much about a woman. I've seldom thought about such things but it did make me think. What would it be like to be married to Mr H.? He wants his things just so, even if it means leaving his room in a mess, and he doesn't take any nonsense. Martha said she wouldn't be Mrs H. for a thousand pounds and I said what about two thousand? We laughed and laughed. I do sometimes wonder if he ever gets lonely now that the doctor is married. Inspector Lestrade once said he wouldn't be surprised if Mr H. was lonely but if he is, he's only got himself to blame. I thought that was unkind. I knew what he meant, but still.

18 July

Very strange and secretive happenings today. I have the cards in front of me of two very distinguished and honourable gentlemen that every person in the country would recognise.[32] *I also have the card of the wife of one of the gentlemen,*[33] *only she visited separately and in the afternoon. What would Mme Charpentier say if she knew I had all three here under my roof in the same day? Well, she will never find out, it seems. The good doctor visited me this evening before he left, to say that under no circumstances should I reveal their presence here today. Good as my word, the three cards are going on the fire right now. I suppose that all will be revealed in good time. All that I can say is that one of them has visited here before and, knowing Mr H., will do so again.*

31 November

I was thinking today of that odd fellow Mr Jankewicz who recently took a room on the top floor. What he got up to, I'll never know, but talk about a night owl. He was in his room all day and then, quite late at night, I'd hear him go out. He was always wearing a long coat and a homburg hat and carrying a bag. I often used to see him in the corridor at eleven, just as I was closing my door at night. None of my business, obviously – but what was his business?

I must say he was always very pleasant and polite, and once helped me when I got the flue brush stuck up the chimney. Bit of

---

32 Could this be Gilbert and Sullivan? I think not.

33 On second thoughts, it could be.

a mystery though and I've enough of those with the comings and goings of Mr H. and the doctor.

One day, the police arrived and for once it wasn't for Mr H. Two constables demanded entry and bustled past his rooms and went up to the second floor. Down they came with Mr Jankewicz. He smiled at me, thanked me for my hospitality and said that he hoped we'd meet again.

I asked other landladies what they'd heard, but nothing. However, Hannah told me this morning that she'd read of a poor man found floating in the Thames wearing an astrakhan coat and homburg, but that could be any number of gentlemen. I still wonder about him.[34]

22 December

To Cavanaugh's Music Hall, with Hannah.

Bella Lomax has returned from New York with new songs,[35] *a new wig and a new husband. I think this one is a doctor. Not that it means she's one to avoid trouble, as there was quite a stir in the front row this evening. I don't know what the gentleman concerned was thinking, but there he was, bold as brass, jumping up on stage trying to dance with poor old Bella.*

---

34 Jaroslav Jankewicz, a Polish émigré, was released by the police after question-ing during the Ripper enquiries. As something of an amateur Ripperologist myself, I can only see Jankewicz as a red herring. It seems fairly obvious that the famous jockey, Aiden MacGinty, was the Ripper. Quite why people need to speculate any further is beyond me.

35 A playbill of the period reveals the following additions to the Lomax portfolio: 'Billy the Kid is the boy for me'; 'A cow and three acres' (alternate title: 'Three acres and a cow') and 'Diddle diddle dumpling (my son John)'.

I should say that it is not unheard of for Bella to dance with a member of the audience, but that is always much later on, after Bella has had a chance to gargle with some brandy – which she calls her cough mixture.

Do you know what? Hannah nearly missed the whole thing as she got up to excuse herself halfway through 'Your Father Never Told You 'Cos Your Mother Never Would'. Odd, I thought, as it's one of her favourites. She was back in time to see what happened.

Back to this poor lad, ruddy faced and in his best bib and tucker, who began his advances by singing along with Bella. She was not impressed, I can tell you. Every time he tried to finish a line, she changed the words. Very funny. And then, when he began to climb onto the stage (with beer bottle in hand, I might add) Bella did her famous little-girl act. She twirled her ringlets and shouted something into the wings that a little girl would never say. And to think that in days of old she would have joined in. Unfortunately, he found no such welcome on stage. As he was dragged away to the back of the stalls he even made a complaint that Bella sent him a note! The very thought. How we laughed! We saw the gentleman in question a while later. Talk about two lovely black eyes. I don't think he'll be interrupting Bella's act again.

She really is a marvel and one only hopes that she graces us for longer in these dark times.

The mood was lifted considerably when we all sang 'Gladstone's Pen is Full of Ink'.

Much Ripper talk on the way home made us thankful that Hannah's nephew, Marcus, was there to walk us home.

23 December

Christmas visit with the Brayleys. As she handed me another ivy ribbon (honestly, that is six she has given me already) Hannah confessed to me that she had written the note at Cavanaugh's. Cheeky thing. Happy Christmas!

Page 164 torn out of *The Martyrdom of Man* by Winwood Reade, annotated by John Watson, with an additional note at the bottom by Sherlock Holmes. Date unknown. Possibly 1872.

J. W.'s notes at the top: 'Morstan. Mary. Governess. Daughter of a Captain. Indian Regiment. 27? Blue eyes.'

The wife was at first a domestic animal like a dog or a horse. She could not be used without the consent of the proprietor but he was always willing to let her out for hire. Among savages it is usually the duty of the host to lend a wife to his stranger guest, and if the loan is declined the husband considers himself insulted. Adultery is merely a question of debt. The law of debt is terribly severe: the body of the insolvent belongs to the creditor to sell or to kill. But no other feelings are involved in the question. The injured husband is merely a creditor, and is always pleased that the debt has been incurred. Petitioner and co-respondent may often be seen smoking a friendly pipe together after the case has been proved and the money has been paid. However, as the intelligence expands and the sentiments become more refined, marriage is hallowed by religion; adultery is regarded as a shame to the husband, and a sin against the gods; and a new feeling – Jealousy – enters for the first time the heart of man. The husband desires to monopolise his wife, body and soul. He intercepts her glances; he attempts to penetrate into her thoughts. He covers her with clothes; he hides even her face from the public gaze. His jealousy, not only anxious for the future, is extended over the past. Thus women from their earliest childhood are subjected by the selfishness of man to severe but salutary laws. Chastity becomes the rule of female life. At first it is preserved by force alone. Male slaves are appointed to guard the women who, except sometimes from momentary pique, never betray one another, and are allied against the men.

J. W. – A remarkable book, made all the more remarkable by your decision to remove this page to write notes upon. I return it forthwith from the isolation of the bureau to complete your understanding of the Bedouin. S. H.

1889

29 July

Before I served tea and coffee to Mr H., Dr W. and their visitor Mr Phelps this morning, Mr H. came downstairs to request that I serve him curried chicken, to serve ham and eggs to Dr Watson but to withhold Mr Phelps's breakfast and deliver an empty plate instead. When I asked Mr H. why, he said nothing but gave me a little cylinder of blue paper to hide under Phelps's cover. I just hope Mr Phelps doesn't eat that – what larks!

Having done what he asked and upon my return, Mr H. said that my breakfast is as good as any Scotswoman's. Why he said that, I'll never know. Another mystery.

As I left, I heard quite a commotion and then Dr Watson calling down for brandy on account of Mr Phelps nearly fainting.

I said to the doctor that my curried chicken usually produces this reaction, but he was too distracted by events upstairs to laugh at my little joke. I told Hannah later on and she laughed.

CURRIED CHICKEN

1 chicken, 2oz of butter, 2 large onions sliced, 1 apple, 1 pint of gravy, 1 dessertspoonful of curry powder, 1 tablespoonful of flour, 4 tablespoons of cream, ½ pint of gravy and 1 tablespoonful of lemon-juice.

Slice the onions and then peel, core and chop your apple before cutting the chicken into equal joints. Put the butter into a pan along with the peeled, cored and minced apple. Fry this until brown and add the stock, before stewing gently for twenty minutes. Mix the curry powder and the flour with a little of the gravy and stir this into the pan. Let it simmer for half an hour, and then add the cream and lemon-juice. Serve with boiled rice.

Dr Watson often likes me to add some shallots with shavings of little garlic.

4 October

Here's a thing. This morning, we arranged for a hansom to take Dr Watson to Paddington. Mr H. had his face on – I call it his 'case face'. Normally this means that he is excited, but for some reason, after the doctor left, he seemed troubled. I wondered what was going on. Well, when Mr H. went out this afternoon, he left a book behind. Not that I'm one to be nosey but I noticed it was called Crossing's Wanderings and Adventures on Dartmoor *and it was open on a page about a family called Baskerville, who lived there. I remember that this was the name of the gentleman who was here earlier in the week – I have his card. Hannah was with me and she said that she would like to play detective. So she read further and we saw some pencil marks on a bit about a dog.*

I could not make head nor tail of it, I can tell you, and nor could Hannah. We wondered why Mr Holmes and Dr Watson had not gone together but before we could wonder any more, Mr H. came back to retrieve his book. He looked down at the book and then up at us, and smiled.

'Don't worry Mrs Hudson,' he said. 'Dr Watson is quite safe.'

I believed him. There's more goes on in that head than we will ever know.

14 October

Although Dr Watson has moved out, he seems to still be living here. I will ask him in the morning what his intentions are. Mr Disraeli has gone missing.

15 October

Still no sign of Mr Disraeli.

23 October

Mr Disraeli has met his end. I saw him in Baker Street chasing a cat called Napoleon who had stolen a fish. Mr Disraeli was killed trying to outrun a cab that had got in his way. Billy has buried him in the yard and Martha sang a song about a fishing boat she'd remembered from school. He died nobly, trying to battle a villain. Mr H. would have been proud.

1890

1 January

It is nearly ten years since I began writing a diary and nearly ten years since Mr Holmes moved in. Every day seems to bring a new challenge stranger than the last. I suppose if they made sense, Mr H. would be out of a job.

16 November

Mr H. has been working at a case down at Rotherhithe and he came back today looking quite terrible. White as a sheet he was and, with not so much as a sound, he took to his bed. I can't say I'll ever get used to his manner, but I am a little worried when it prevents him getting some help.

17 November

Mr H. often stays in his room for a whole morning but today I was understandably concerned when he didn't appear. When Mrs Brayley's nephew, Marcus, returned with the navy from the

Caribbean last year, he left me some Warburg's Fever Tincture.[36] *I climbed the stairs this afternoon to offer Mr H. some but there was not even a response. This is more than worrying. If only the doctor were here. He would know what to do. I shall insist in the morning that I fetch a doctor. I don't think I shall sleep much tonight.*

18 November

Mr H. said he would not let me get a doctor at first when I persisted this morning, but thank heavens he eventually let me fetch Dr Watson. There was no other way to put this but I thought he was dying. For three days now he's had neither food nor drink and he has been sinking fast. This morning I saw his bones sticking out of his face and his great bright eyes, now dimmed, looking at me. I doubted he would last the day. I could stand no more of it and thought that now the disease was taking hold, I must do something about it.

I returned with Dr Watson, who wasted no time in going up to

---

36 Warburg's Fever Tincture was a fever medicine that is no longer readily available. It was developed in 1834 by German physician Dr Carl Warburg. His tincture was very popular at the time, however, I consider it to be inferior to quinine. I happen to be a keen amateur tropical disease specialist and have managed to identify Holmes's fever as a melioidosis or a rare form of TB known as Vietnamese tuberculosis. I feel confident that Dr Watson would have come to the same conclusion had he been given the chance. Instead, he probably made the rather snap judgement that it is some sort of coolie disease from Sumatra. The coughing, weight loss, fatigue and fever may indeed lead one to this conclusion, naive as it may sound, but an analysis of the bloody vomit, aching upper back, sleeplessness and clear signs of iron deficient related ennui would point the good doctor in my direction. How people die of it and how many a year is an area I am keen to follow up on (note to self: new book?), given that early signs give the number of potential fatalities to be as much as 200,000.

his old rooms to talk to his stubborn friend. Immediately there were raised voices and even an almighty cry from Mr H. – I thought that there must be some hope.

I have to say I did not behave very well when Dr Watson came down, and I must confess to having shed some tears. However, things moved so quickly afterwards that I didn't know what to think.

Dr Watson returned with a Mr Culverton Smith. And then Inspector Morton followed. Then there was a crash and a scuffle and Mr Culverton Smith was led out. All in a matter of minutes.

Mr H. and the doctor followed a little while later and would you believe it, Mr H. was in fine fettle with not a trace of his former complaint. Rather than explaining events to me, he merely asked for supper to be cancelled as he would be dining at Simpson's. I was left none the wiser and not a little unhappy, I can tell you. Next time he's at death's door, he might have the decency to tell me. After today's events, I think I'll need some medication myself and probably more than one.

28 December

I prepared a woodcock for Mr H. and the doctor as agreed, and then they both hurry out of the door without so much as a by-your-leave. I wouldn't mind only I spent the best part of an afternoon cleaning a goose for Mr H. and he immediately gave that away to a loony in a scotch bonnet. Merry Christmas indeed!

Initially, I thought this was a picture of Mrs Hudson herself, but the signature on the back seems to give a lie to this. I confess your humble researcher was at a loss to determine its origin of such a name but, nothing daunted, I pursued the quest and noticed a strong resemblance to another photograph. This, I had discovered was a distant relative of Mrs Hudson, Charlotte Kirby, who had moved to the Outer Hebrides where she had married a crofter. Nevertheless, who was the 'Michaelene' scrawled on the reverse?[37] The hunt was on. Such a distinctive name must emerge and, heavens be praised, it did. Michaelene Ferrier was the sister of Charlotte and had a very different life. A brilliant medical student, she qualified and practised in the East End of London as one of the first female GPs in Britain. She became involved in social work among the poor and, due to befriending various (ahem) 'ladies of the night', also came to know some of the criminal class. The details are not clear, but what is an established fact is that she was once arrested in possession of explosives. Around this time, anarchists were active in the area and it is intriguing to speculate how such a socially conscious woman came to embrace such a cause. My research produced the amazing discovery that she became known as 'Fireworks Ferrier – the gelignite girl',[38] and, sad to relate, she finally blew herself up in Southwark. When one realises that Mrs Hudson's husband also suffered a similar combustive end, the coincidence is remarkable. Explosive revelations indeed.

---

37 Why the signature on the photo remains to be seen. I am not perfect, after all.
38 She was operating under this 'nom de guerre' around 1875, the year that Alfred Nobel gave us the aforesaid explosive material.

Mrs Hudson's hiatus 1891–94

1891

2 January

Arthur, please forgive me not writing yesterday. Hannah persuaded me to join her for a jolly new year's trip to Ye Grapes in Shepherd Market and, as you can guess, it was full of her usual tomfoolery. Let me tell you what happened. We were both to be dressed as nuns, she said. I should've asked why but she told me she'd done it before. When we got there, Hannah began telling customers not to enter the pub. I must confess, I felt very proper in my wimple, but I spent most of the time trying not to laugh as she did so. One man stopped to ask us if we'd ever had a drink. Hannah was horrified and said no. He said we shouldn't tell people not to drink if we'd never tried one. Hannah solemnly agreed but said that we could never be seen entering a pub. So, she asked him to bring us the drinks outside in two teacups. With our ears at the door, we heard the man asking for two large whiskeys in teacups. 'Are those nuns out there again?' said the landlord, and we ran away, laughing. Honestly, the nonsense Hannah gets up to and here's me, joining in. Arthur, you would have laughed the loudest, I'm sure. I cannot believe another year has gone by without you, my dear.

5 January

Today I heard the front door go. It must've been off the latch for some reason. I went out into the street, but there was no one there. Anyway, later on, I went in to Mr Holmes's room and there on his desk was a note. I couldn't resist looking. And do you know what it said?

'Army Riot.'

What on earth?

Mr Holmes came in shortly after and came into the kitchen. He asked if anybody had called and I said no, but I heard the door go. He didn't mention the note but somehow I knew it was connected. I've never seen him so disturbed.

Then, this afternoon, Inspector Lestrade stopped by for some tea and I mentioned the note to him. 'Army Riot?' he said. 'What on earth?' Well, that's what I thought, I told him. Then he went very thoughtful and asked for a piece of paper. He wrote 'Army Riot' on it and sat staring at it. Then he wrote all the letters on a newspaper, tore them out and put them in a circle on the table. Then he stared at them, jabbing with his pen. And I thought, what's he up to? 'Ah!' he says, 'it's an anagram, Mrs Hudson. It's an anagram!' He rushed upstairs straight to Mr Holmes with some alarm. Shortly after Moaner left, I popped in with a cup of coffee and found Mr Holmes looking rather gravely at the note and the bits of paper. He asked me if I had seen anyone come in and when I said no, he sat, gazing out of the window as if I wasn't there, with a look I had never seen before. What had Moaner said?[39]

12 March

I've just returned from Glasshouse Street, not far from the Cambrian Stores. There, I spied a mob – not unusual for the Cambrian at this time of night – and they were gathered around a tussle – again, not unusual – so I walked over to take a closer look.

I was greeted by the sight of two women punching each other. Quite what the argument was, I had no idea. There was certainly no love lost between the two of them and I turned to the gentleman next to me and asked what was going on. He told me that a maid called Nellie Bowman had taken a shine to another woman's husband and this was the result. Apparently it started in the pub and only now had spilled out into the street. Well, the landlord of the pub, Al Perkins (who I know from his boxing days as Piccadilly Perkins) suggested a ring be marked out in the street and the problem be solved there. He even offered to referee but his place had already been taken by the old Chinaman with one eye from Berwick Street. His job was made difficult by the fact that a dog spent most of the bout trying to jump up at the two women. I

---

39 I have reread the entire Holmes canon and can find no trace of an army riot. However, once I employed Inspector Lestrade's rather innovative method for solving anagrams, I was able to abstract the following name. I can now confidently state that Mary Trio must be the suspect we are looking for. Case solved.

wish I could have stayed longer but it was getting late. When I left, the Salvation Army band had arrived and was trying to calm the situation by playing 'What a friend we have in Jesus'. Handsome takings at the pub, I should think.

It has been a long time since I saw a boxing match but apparently Jock Reid (son of Hamish Reid – 'The Celtic Claymore') has decided to come out of retirement again to fight Jasper Winstanley ('The Chelsea Snob') at the Barracks on Friday. I am sorely tempted and wonder whether Hannah will join me.

20 March

Mrs Flint from Dorset Street gave birth to triplets last night. Half the street turned up this afternoon as it is such a rare thing. Herbert Flint went to wet the babies heads and hasn't been seen since.

23 April

St George's Day. A day to forget. I am writing this from Mrs Brayley's kitchen. Martha is asleep upstairs, Billy is staring into the fire with the most horrible look upon his face and Hannah is scrambling around in the larder looking for some gin. I can barely write I am trembling so, I am just delighted to be able to write at all. Earlier this afternoon, I heard the door open with a crack and heavy feet pounded upstairs followed by shouting, struggling and the sound of breaking glass. I was confronted in the hall by a man, whose horrible face I will never forget for as long as I live, who charged past me and up the stairs with a flaming torch. To my horror, I saw Billy having it out with two more burly types at the top of the stair and I feared he might be thrown down but, to his credit, he managed to chase them off. The man with the torch was stronger and got himself into Mr Holmes's room before setting fire to the curtains. Thank goodness for Martha – she had already run into the street to sound the alert and it was not long before the engine and the men with their lamps and hoses were there to prevent a final catastrophe. Who would do such a thing?

24 April

Hannah is such a good friend. To take us all in as she did last night was very kind. We were able to return this afternoon and I'm happy to say that all was not as bad as we first feared. Thankfully, Mr Holmes and Dr Watson have not returned yet but, until they do, we'll not know why this has happened. Billy has set to work straight away repairing things and even Inspector Gregson came round to let me know that the culprits won't get away. Another sleepless night I fear.

25 April

Baked Hannah a very special cake today as a thank you.

TIPSY CAKE

Put 4lb of castor sugar into a basin with 2 tablespoonfuls of sugar, 1 pinch of salt and the yolks of seven eggs; beat the mixture well, then gradually sift in 5oz of flour. Whip the whites of eight eggs, mix with the batter and pass the whole mixture through a hair sieve. Take a warm mould and grease it with fat, dusting it with some caster sugar. Fill the mould three parts with the batter, put it on a hot baking-sheet and bake it for an hour. When cooked, turn the cake on to a sieve and leave it till it has cooled. Cut out a round of Genoa cake, about 2in. thick and bake it in a flat stew pan. Coat the cake with orange icing, place it on a dish and put the Savoy cake in the centre. Make holes in some oranges and empty them of juice and pulp. Put some butter in the holes and place the oranges on ice. Fill the oranges with alternate layers of blancmange and red orange-jelly. When the mixture is solid, divide them into quarters from top to bottom, cut an end off each of the quarters so that they will stand upright, surround the Savoy cake with the imitation oranges and serve.

I had to borrow a little of Mr H.'s Madeira wine too! Hannah did enjoy herself.

4 May

I don't know why, but something made me go up to the first floor today. I wondered whether Mr Holmes had come back without telling me. Billy has finished the new wallpaper and it is as if nothing had happened. The funniest thing struck me as I was in that room. A cold wind suddenly blew in from the window and made me shiver. It felt as if there was somebody there for a moment, but no. I locked the door quite quickly and have decided I won't go upstairs until we know they're back.

7 May

The most dreadful news. A man describing himself as Mr H.'s brother[40] greeted me in my own kitchen this morning clutching a piece of paper. It was a news wire about an accident involving Mr H. and another man. It said that he had been killed. I was so upset that I couldn't speak, but the strangest thing was that this man didn't seem too put out. Instead, he told me that I was to keep Mr H.'s rooms locked until further notice and was on no account to touch his things. He also asked that I'm to let Wiggins know if anybody calls for Mr H. I offered to open the rooms up so he could attend to matters himself but he declined and left soon after. This is all very strange. If it were my brother, I may have behaved differently but I've heard he has his own way. This is all too terrible and I don't know what to think.

14 May

Still no word from the doctor. Where can he be? A package arrived from Mr H.'s brother and inside was a year's worth of rent. Something is not right.

16 May

I hear the doctor has returned. Thank heavens. Mrs Watson must have been worried sick.

---

40 Mycroft Holmes, obviously.

10 July

Dr Watson has still not visited but I cannot blame him. Mrs Gresham, who visited his practice last week, told me that he wasn't there. The maid informed her that all the doctor does is sit in his study at home and write. In fact, my heart leapt when I heard movement on the stairs yesterday but it was only old Moaner. He'd come to pay his respects. Times are a little lean for the poor man now that Mr H. is gone. I asked if there was anything I could do to help but he just shrugged his shoulders and left. Didn't stay for a cup of tea or anything. Poor lamb. Pity, as he missed Mr H.'s brother by a whisker. Not sure about Mr H.'s brother at all. He has visited a few times now and the situation is still no clearer.

2 September

Dear Arthur,

I'm sorry I haven't written for some weeks now but life here at 221b is just not the same now Mr H. is gone. His brother has stopped visiting and I do not know whether or not to open his room again. The doctor is by the coast and cannot be reached. You would know what to do, my sweet. For now, I must wait.

29 December

There was a noise in Mr Holmes's room this afternoon. Who could it be? There are only three keys to the rooms. I have one. The doctor has one and Mr Holmes had the other. Well, Mr Mycroft Holmes can keep his instructions. I decided to open up the room.

I unlocked the door and everything was in its place. Well, I say everything, save O'Connell[41] *tugging at a Persian slipper by the fireside. How did he get in there? One thing is certain: Mr Holmes would have worked it out.*

---

41 As you will of course remember, O'Connell is the surviving member of the cat community at 221b. He must be ten years old by now. A good age for a cat of his type.

This is a true novelty. Mrs Hudson may even have taken it herself.[42] It's the butcher's shop where D. L. worked. The letters above the shop are, at first sight, indecipherable, hidden as they are by tarpaulin. However, I have deduced, from the visible ones, 'K.R.I.C.'. This is almost certainly the shop of Vladimir Pukric, a Russian immigrant and pioneer kosher butcher. I say almost, because Mrs Hudson refers to Mr Yarrow as being the butcher, but I have to disagree. The man may well be Mr Pukric, but the woman is certainly not his wife as he was known to be a confirmed bachelor. This fact, coupled with his ethnicity, led to his becoming something of a gregarious recluse – open and expansive whilst serving his customers, but living alone with his butterfly collection out of working hours. A poignant picture, hinting at the pathos of a butcher behind closed doors, who rarely came out to 'meat' his fellows.[43] The wicker baskets are typical of butcher's assistants at this time but the gentlemen sporting such ample examples do not appear to be in the least bit connected to butchery.

---

42 Perhaps with a Box Brownie?
43 Please delete this unworthy pun.

Mrs Hudson's hiatus
by Oliver Philpott

A considered view of the years 1892–94

*J*feel it is my duty to step in at this point
and explain a little about the background to
the two-year period titled 'Mrs Hudson's hiatus'.
The devotees of Holmes like to refer to this period in
Sherlock's life as The Great Hiatus, in which he is said
to have travelled the world. He spent two years in Tibet,
had an amusing visit to Lhasa (where he visited the head
Lama no less), posed as a Norwegian explorer named
Sigerson, then went through Persia, Mecca and paid a
short but interesting visit to the Khalifa at Khartoum,
before returning to France where he spent some months
researching coal-tar derivatives in a laboratory at
Montpelier. Just as Dr Watson appears to have picked
up his pen with renewed vigour during this period, it

seems Mrs Hudson did precisely the opposite. No diary entries were found for 1892 or 1893.

Some might consider it futile to speculate on her movements during this time, but you know I can leave no mystery intriguingly unsolved. In fact, as something of an amateur (as in 'lover of', I should add) graphologist, I embarked upon an analysis of our good lady's handwriting to see if I could open a window into her patterns of behaviour. Incidentally, I can offer my services in the complementary field of Graphotherapy – please see my website www.philpottsworld.com for details ('You too, can make the "write" change!'[44]). For those of you familiar with the engrossing art of graphology, you'll be pleased to know that my analysis of Mrs Hudson's handwriting focuses mainly on the major cardinal traits of the language of ink – namely the Slant, the Space, the Baseline, the Flex, the Swoop, the Elision, the Halt (controversially), the Size, the Signature (everyone's favourite!) and the Serif, not to mention the foot soldiers of our trade: the Capitalisations and the Exclamatories. To begin with, Mrs Hudson's sloping h's give us the impression of someone who is constant and yet curious. Perhaps she may have travelled in her mind during this time, if not in her deeds. Unfortunately, nowhere in the diaries does Mrs Hudson's signature manifest itself. It was upon investigating her vacillations and true

---

44 Enough of the sales pitch! – Publisher

ascending baseline that this thought struck me. Without this crucial piece of evidence, my graphological analysis reached something of a stalemate.

However, not to be deterred and mindful that what follows might make me seem like something of a fruitless pontificator, my supporting analysis did present the following theories:

The diaries yield seven instances of the word 'Scotch', therefore, Mrs Hudson may have upped sticks and moved to Scotland for two years. The fact that she never mentions living in Scotland in any way, shape or form did not deter this most tenacious of bloodhounds. However, it is unlikely.

She may have gone wandering in the Serengeti. I base this on the fact that, following the resumption of her writing, she mentions the warm weather quite a bit. Perhaps she was now used to hotter temperatures?

Perhaps she became a nun in Western Ireland? I had an aunt who was a nun in Western Ireland and she used to use the words 'lawks' as well. I cannot entirely rule this out, no matter how tempting.

She was kidnapped following Sebastian Moran's attack. Why not? She wouldn't be the first associate of Holmes to have this fate befall them. However, it's highly unlikely given her handwriting post-hiatus shows no sign of being hindered by the recent presence of manacles.

She ran off with D. L. We know she didn't because she says explicitly that this didn't happen, but it doesn't stop it being a theory. After all, Holmes himself said that when you have eliminated the impossible, whatever remains, however improbable, must be the truth. However, this is both impossible and improbable.

She posed as a Norwegian explorer named Sigerson.

But despite all of these theories, I have decided to discount them all in favour of the following:

She did continue writing, but these parts of the diaries have yet to be found. A shocking conclusion, I think you'll agree. Maybe someone like Moriarty stole them? Maybe he was looking for recipes? It is well known that he had a weakness for chocolate-coated madeleines.[45] If only our esteemed consulting detective had known this fact, then he could have brought the whole affair of The Final Problem to a much earlier conclusion, without the need for those Reichenbach shenanigans. Upon their first meeting, a carefully placed plate of this small shell-like buttery delicacy from north-eastern France could have distracted the Napoleon of crime, perhaps giving Holmes an opportunity to exploit this most obvious of Achilles heels! Food-related fatal flaws in criminal masterminds are not unknown.

Who can forget Hannibal Lecter's penchant for his victim's liver, accompanied by some fava beans and a nice Chianti? I certainly can't! A little grizzlier than a chocolate covered madeleine I grant you, but the

---

45 Really? – Publisher

structure holds. In fact I confess that I have been known to do rather a good impression of this most sinister of nemeses. Just last autumn, I found myself fashioning a facemask from the most simple of household objects, a colander and a dog collar (sans dog of course). Utilising a supermarket trolley (which I did return incidentally – those pound coins don't grow on trees!) and wheeled in by a willing friend, local dentist Neil Hawes, bless him, I made quite the splash at a number of functions that year. I even interrupted the reading of the minutes at the local Rotarian AGM, with my now famous cry of, 'Tell me, Clarice – have the lambs stopped screaming?' It seemed to go down quite well considering they'd only just been paying tribute to our recently deceased Mayor, Tony Sedgwick. I like to think that had he been able to be there, Tony would have enjoyed the whole thing. Whenever I pass the lock gates where he disappeared, I often like to utter his own famous cry of 'Daddy's here!' by way of tribute. He'll be missed by all, particularly by the staff at the Hinchley Wood Harvester.

But only when we find the chocolate thumbprints on the missing pages can we say for certain that this theory is conclusive. In the meantime, I think we've all had some sport and I'm just delighted to have been your captain. The whistle blows! Time for the second half...

III

The landlady returns 1894–1903

1894

1 January

I woke up today in a cheery mood. I do not know why. Well, here I am writing my diary again.

1 March

To the New Royal[46] for a spot of cakes, ale and singing. Bella Lomax has returned from Europe and is a little larger than I remember. She must be twenty-two stone but is still as dainty as a sprite.[47] She is with the same husband. We were glad to see her back – I suspect he was too. She was reported to have had lunch with the Prince Regent whilst in Paris and his lunches are

---

46 The famous Music Hall at 242 High Holborn, formerly known as Weston's. Readers will be interested to note that Weston's was next door to Gilligan & Sons, at the time London's most fashionable undertakers. Clients included Lord Lonsdale.

47 The mind boggles.

legendary.[48] *Billy and I sang our hearts out during her new one —* '*Put Your Feather in my Titfer*'.

New Royal Songsheet
PUT YOUR FEATHER IN MY TITFER
Music by George Langdon Words by Percy Oldfield[49]

Put your feather in my titfer
When me you want to woo
Put your feather in my titfer
And I'll save a kiss for you
Put your feather in my titfer
And always I'll be true
Put your feather in my titfer
And we'll doodle oodle oo!

48 The less said about them the better.

49 'Put Your Feather in my Titfer' appears to be the only collaboration between these two men. George Langdon went on to become something of a well-regarded classical composer in his own right, penning, among others 'The Croydon Song Cycle' and 'The Margate Fugues'. Percy Oldfield, on the other hand, met with a rather sad end. Details are sketchy, but it appears that 'Put Your Feather in my Titfer' was his high point. Not long afterwards, following a bout of malarial fever, he apparently jumped off London Bridge. Happily, the Titfer song remains as his legacy. Other songs noted by Billy, and found in among the diaries: 'Johnny gave me his ha'penny / So I gave him a bun'; 'Her name was Penny Farthing / So she took him for a ride'; 'When the boys come back from Durban / I'll wave the Union Jack'; 'I'm your sugar, and you're my sweet.'

Bella kept winking at a man in the front row. He was made up about that, I can tell you, slapping his thigh and waving his topper at her. Funny thing is, we didn't see him for the second half – overcome by overexcitement, I shouldn't wonder. Archie Kempton and his Tumbling Pygmies finished the show in great style. On the way home, we sang Bella's new song all the way along the length of Great Portland Street. I am looking forward to our next visit to the New Royal!

3 March

The Grand Old Man resigned today. I never knew what to make of Mr Gladstone.[50] Although he was stern looking, apparently he was a man who used to 'rescue fallen women'. As Hannah said 'Who would fall for him?' – made me laugh. I did feel sorry for those women though, especially with Mr Gladstone looming up out of the darkness. We even get one or two of those girls around here sometimes. One of them knocked on the door one day, asking if a Mr Nash lived here. Apparently he owed her some money. I invited her in for some tea and seed cake. Well, the stories she told me would make your hair curl and the names she came out with – well, I never did. Some of her clients are quite well known but, to look at them, you'd think butter wouldn't melt in their mouths. I won't say too much, but one of them is in Mr Watts's Hall of Fame!

---

50 William Ewart Gladstone was, indeed, known as the Grand Old Man of British politics, which was often shortened to G. O. M. Benjamin Disraeli, upon hearing this acronym, once opined that it stood for 'God's Only Mistake'. There was no love lost there, one can assume.

Hannah said she'd heard of one of the girls going to see a doctor because she was tired out. He assured her she'd soon be on her back again. I can't believe I write these jokes of Hannah's down, but they make me laugh. I can't imagine Mr Gladstone laughing much but Mr Disraeli used to make the Queen laugh, so I've heard. Such a wonderful man. There's one story where the Queen was at dinner with Gladstone and she said afterwards that she thought him the cleverest man in England. When asked about Disraeli, she said that he made her feel like the cleverest woman in England. She'll go on forever.[51]

1 April

I have never, ever, in my life fainted. Today was the exception. The sound of the key in the lock at lunchtime was unmistakable. I thought I'd seen a ghost at first but no, it was him. I confess that I must have made a complete fool of myself, Arthur. I cried like a baby. It is two o'clock now and he is sitting upstairs in his old armchair as if nothing has happened. The doctor is to visit this evening and I must say that I feel the light has returned to Baker Street. Billy has been working hard to open the rooms up again and have things just as our oldest tenant would have them. Mr H.'s return is a wonderful gift.

---

51 Au contraire! In fact she died in 1901.

3 April

I have been living in Baker Street for nearly twenty years now but today, I couldn't believe it, I got lost. The fog had me very confused, I will say, but how I could not get back from Cavendish Square to here, I do not know. Perhaps the excitement of the last few days have made me muddled. I found myself in a small road that led me into Manchester Street and then Blandford Street. I went down a narrow passage that I thought I recognised, and found myself at the back door of a house. I felt someone was following me and I was rather scared. The house was pitch dark and obviously empty, but I swear I heard a floorboard creak from within. I stopped for a moment to get my eyes used to the light and eventually I could see a street lamp. Surely that must be Baker Street, I thought and I was exactly right. The building was Camden House, which stands opposite my own. I rushed across the road and shut the door. The sound of Mr H.'s violin cheered me for a change. It may be April, but I think we may need fires in the morning.

4 April

Mr H. has asked me to do some funny things through the years, but this really took the biscuit. Maybe his time abroad has addled his brain. He asked me to take a look at a dummy he'd made of himself. It gave me quite a start, it was so lifelike. I asked him what he was doing with it and he told me that there was a chance someone might take a pot shot at him, which I thought was dreadful. He was going to put the dummy in the window to fool them. I wondered how they would think it was Mr H., as it wasn't moving about. He gave me one of his rare smiles, congratulated me and asked me to kneel on the floor and move the dummy around to fool people outside. I didn't know what to think. Me with my knees and with a good chance of a bullet to boot? I swear my legs were on the point of giving up by the end. What I do for that man. What will tomorrow's pantomime be?

5 April

Dr Watson has moved back in. The funeral was only last month but his return to his old quarters seems to have brought him some peace.

1 June

Never a dull moment, as they say, whoever they are.[52] The other day I went in to Mr H.'s rooms to lower the blinds and there was an old woman standing there, bold as brass. And none too respectable, by the look of her. I asked her who she was, what she was doing there and how she got in. She said the door was open. I told her it is always locked. Then she laughed and said that she climbed in through the window. Then she started laughing again, fit to burst. I thought about calling the police. This mad woman was in my house! Would you believe it, she then took her hair off and some teeth out of her mouth. It was Mr H.! I had to sit down, so I did. And do you know, he went to my kitchen and made me a

---

52 I think you'll find it was Jerome K. Jerome in 'Three Men in a Boat'. A great favourite of mine.

cup of tea. He's an odd fish. I can't remember that ever happening before but nothing surprises me anymore.

17 October

Hannah has bought a new chaise longue and it won't fit through her front door. When people ask her why it is in the street, she tells them that it is the fashion in Paris.

This would seem to be a promotional picture from the musical burlesque *The Milkmaids*,[53] which had a short run at the Gaiety Theatre in 1893.

On the left is Elaline Branscombe, a promising young singer, who sadly was lost in the sinking of the Titanic in 1912. She was travelling to New York to audition for a musical there, but it was sadly not to be.

On the right is Granville Tebbs, who was also making his name at the time as evidenced by his burgeoning mutton chops. Many have speculated that there was a curse on this show, pointing to the fact that he perished in a fire at his lodgings in 1901. The show itself had a short run, perpetuating the myth of the curse, as the backers withdrew funding and were subsequently charged with fraud.

Mrs Hudson was known as an *habitué* of the music hall, rather than of musicals, but she may well have seen this show, although she does not refer to it in her diaries.

Tebbs was often depicted with a churn in hand, the churn featuring in the song 'You were Maid for me, my love', which gained brief popularity and was in fact sometimes sung by Alexandra Fortesque (the Norwood Nightingale) in her musical act. One wonders if she changed the words to 'I'm the Maid for you, my love'. Alexandra also had a sad end, when she perished in a ballooning accident in mid-Sussex.

All in all, the picture does not serve to conjure up happy thoughts. It serves as a reminder of the theatrical scene of the time.

---

53 A real horse appeared on the stage pulling a milk dray.

1895

23 April

Mr H. returned from the country today with a cut lip and a lump upon his forehead. At first I was worried that someone had assaulted him but I found him in good spirits, even laughing when he told me what happened. In the course of his investigation, he had got into a fight in a pub down there after he had endured a string of abuse from a Mr Woodley, who followed this up with a vicious backhander that Mr H. had failed to spot.

I never realised that he is something of a boxer. He never realised that I was something of a boxing fan. When I told him that backhanders are a common tactic of country fighters and the most obvious response is a straight left, he was genuinely taken aback. It is a rare thing to see Mr H. so surprised, but he then admitted he did throw a left. Apparently, Mr Woodley went home in a cart. Wait until I inform Hannah of this. Maybe we will even see Mr H. boxing at Whitechapel one day.

2 May

Moaner finished his chat with Mr H. this evening and came into the kitchen to return my matches. He then produced a packet that he put on the table and asked me to guess what kitchen item it might be. I looked at it and thought that because it was smaller than a wine bottle and a little bigger than an egg cup, it must be a sugar shaker. He looked rather disappointed as he opened the packet to reveal the very thing. He then told me that this was a gift, courtesy of The Yard, for the shaker of mine that he had broken when he visited last week. I was quite touched, I can tell you, and I wasn't going to ask how he came by it, until he told me. Apparently it was reclaimed from the scene of the murder of an opium dealer, where it had been used to hold some poison. He assured me it had been thoroughly cleaned and, even though I believed him, I have put it in the cupboard drawer I reserve for mouse bait.

1896

4 November

*A package arrived this morning and I don't think I've ever seen
Mr H. so cheerful. When I asked him why he was so happy, do
you know what he said as he ran up the stairs? 'It's all because of
a landlady and a bottle of poison!' I spent the rest of the morning
thinking that he was talking about me and the sugar shaker.*

*It was only when I spoke to Dr Watson this afternoon that I
found out he wasn't. The other week, Mr H. had a landlady called
Mrs Merrilow come over to see him from south Brixton.*[54] *I confess*

---

54 Dr Watson is referring to a district called Brixton that sits in the London bor-
ough of Lambeth. The earliest settlement here was shaped by two Roman
roads, Clapham Road (the current A3) and Brixton Road (now better known,
especially in my house, as the A23), and the gateway to God's Own Town that
is Crawley. In the eleventh century it was known as Brixistane, which over the
years became shortened to Brixton (naturally). It underwent a huge change in
the 1880s and 1890s, as trams and railways connected the town with London.
In fact, it is interesting to note that 1880 brought the name Electric Avenue to
Brixton. It was so named after it became the first street to be lit by electricity.
Permit me a personal note – as the popular musical artiste Eddy Grant sang
in the 1980s, 'I'm gonna rock down to Electric Avenue' (I have only recently
embraced the lilting ethnic rhythms of reggae).

I'd never heard of her, though she seemed nice enough. She'd told Mr Holmes and Dr Watson about that awful business with the Ronder family and that lion in Berkshire. As usual, Mr H. solved the case. The doctor told me that the bottle of poison was a gift from Mrs Ronder to let Mr H. know that she was not going to take her own life. The poor woman felt so guilty for her part in her husband's death. How awful, but how proud I am of my lodger. Dr Watson says that even he is surprised by Mr H. sometimes.

1897

23 June

Yesterday was our beloved Queen's Diamond Jubilee. I left Billy in charge of the house and strolled with Hannah to Constitution Hill. Billy didn't mind too much as Annie was visiting. I don't think we'll ever see the like of this Jubilee again. I certainly hope not as it took forever and a day to get anywhere. When Her Majesty passed by, the cheering was quite deafening, and I think everyone was having a lovely time. I walked home with Mrs B. and we stopped to toast Her Majesty's health. There was free ale and tobacco thanks to Mr Lipton, and the Red Lion was open until two o'clock in the morning. I didn't think Hannah would be able to help me in the parlour today! When I returned home, I noticed that Mr Holmes has remained in his room the entire day. When I took him some coffee, I asked him why he had not been on the streets celebrating with everyone else and all he said was, 'Lest we forget, Mrs Hudson, lest we forget.' That is something I've been thinking about all day.

17 September

D. L. has returned but Mr Yarrow said he won't be coming back to work. I suppose all the letters in Somerset have been delivered. For some reason I decided to increase my order with Mr Yarrow and included some pork chops for myself. As a treat.

PORK CHOPS

Fry the chops and leave in a dish by the fire. Lightly cook some onions in the still hot frying pan and then set aside with the chops. Add some flour and then some water to the pan to make a sauce.

20 September

I thought that I spied D. L. in Covent Garden today but I was much mistaken. There was a gentleman hunched over a barrow trying to lift some parsnips into a crate and for some reason his shoulders looked just like D. L.'s and the jacket, too. I thought 'that's even his tweed if I'm not mistaken'. Well, I was mistaken. Can't be helped. I did buy some lovely lilies for the hallway though, but I've had to move them to the parlour as Billy keeps sneezing. I saw one of those electric cabs[55] in Seven Dials on my way back home. It nearly

---

55 The first London horseless carriage taxi was introduced by a man called Walter C. Bersey, who was General Manager of the London Electric Cab Company, situated in Juxon Street, Lambeth, on 19 August 1897. They were known as 'hummingbirds' by the public. After a spate of accidents, police stopped licensing this type of electric cab in 1900. Who would've thought that electric cars would be so 'current' today? Not I!

ran over a horse. They're a terrible thing, the speeds they go at. It was dreadful news about that poor cabbie who crashed one in Bond Street last week.[56]

---

56 Driver George Smith was only fined £1! A sadly familiar trend that still persists today.

1898

10 July

I found this note on Mr Holmes's armchair when I went up to change the linen.

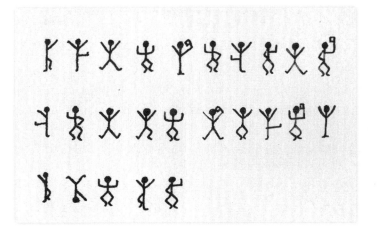

He said I could keep it. I think they are rather jolly.

11 July

Hannah told me that D. L. is working for Mr Yarrow again.

22 July

Arthur, I visited your brother George today. Sally was there with baby Peter and the girls but John was not there on account of a fire in one of Blackfield's print houses. Clerkenwell has changed quite a bit, but George hasn't. He tells me that he is learning to speak Italian so he can understand his neighbours. It's been a long time since Mary died but the poor man struggles on. That niece and nephew of yours have kept his spirits up, though, and he says he is well cared for. He even gave me a prayer book to take home which he had bound himself. Those fingers of his could not take another day stitching a book I was sure of it, but there it was – such lovely work. He asked if I would like to stay and watch Jack Gillespie lose his latest fight up in Shoreditch, but I told him that I'd seen Jack Gillespie lose enough fights, thank you very much, and it was time I let someone else do it.

Martha told me that D. L. came to the door earlier, looking very sheepish and turned on his heels very quickly once he'd delivered. Wouldn't you just know it – he comes and I'm not here.

Sgr Ingnatius Paloma

Lady Sigerson

MONS. VERTUS PUGILUM

Count Von Kramm

Fighting near the Maritsani
The relief of Mafeking
Monday 18 June 1900

It was then 4.45 and a bewildering moment for the Brigadier, who had a great bulky convoy to protect and had it at the moment in a defenceless position. I think I would not take any reward to bear the responsibility of acting at such a moment. The shots were sounding quicker, but one could see nothing except the surrounding trees. Colonel Mahon looked coolly round. 'We must try with the guns,' he said, and ordered another squadron out on the right. The convoy was moving on now as broad a front as the shrubs and trees would permit; it raised a cloud of dust, which the level rays of the sun lit like a rainbow, and the bullets began to come in a hail. There was no cover; everyone was under fire; so there was nothing to do but to dismount and lead one's horse along beside the convoy. Every now and then among the clear high 'phit' of the Mauser bullet would come the hideous twisting whistle of the Martini – really a horrible sound. There was something like a panic amongst the native drivers; they walked along bent almost double, taking what shelter they could; one I saw crawling along on his belly, and the sight made me laugh, although I had at heart too much sympathy with him to be really amused. In his capacity for the Morning Post Winston C

This cutting (incomplete – grr!) would seem to be from Holmes's famous index file and has found its way into our Aladdin's cave. As you can see, it refers to the Second Boer War (which began in 1899) and, in a giant leap to more recent times, there is a reference to a Winston at the bottom. Winston Churchill was a war correspondent and was captured during the conflict. Why had Holmes kept this cutting? We may never know. Was there a link with the young Winston Churchill? I went to work and, lo and behold, at the end of the cutting there is a 'C' after the word Winston. How many Winstons were there at the time? There cannot have been that many.[57] Churchill didn't hold government office until 1905 when he was appointed Under Secretary for the colonies, then President of the Board of Trade and then Home Secretary in 1911. It was during this tenure that he was present at the famous 'Siege of Sydney Street' and, when I ploughed on with my research into his career, I realised that it was out of the compass of this book. Ah well, that's enough *cutting* remarks! Nevertheless I like to indicate these points of interest as we travel along the highways and byways of the period, whether relevant or not.[58]

---

57 Well, why don't you find out? – Publisher
58 In that case, this irrelevance should be DELETED. – Publisher

1899

23 January

D. L. and I were able to take advantage of the first bright day of the year and walked to the Serpentine. He is very good company and seems back to his old self. He talks a lot of the future and I had to remind him that he is in his fifties and perhaps he should be thinking more of making a home for himself. There were many soldiers in the park and D. L. found himself asking them questions about the Cape. His spirits lifted when we met John Campbell, the landlord of The Crown, and his young family. D. L. lights up when he sees the Campbell boys and it's as if he is still chasing around the factory floor when he plays with them. I left them as the sun faded as Martha is attending a dance practice this evening in preparation for the Regent's Park Burns' Night Supper. Much leg twisting.

FREE FARMS FOR THE MILLION IN THE BEAUTIFUL PROVINCE OF

Manitoba and Canadian North West

have 150,000,000 acres of the best Wheat Land in the world, and 50,000,000 acres of the best Grazing; Land.

RAILWAY COMMUNICATION

Open to all parts of the Continent. The Canada Pacific is now running about 900 miles west of Winnipeg, and has now reached the summit of the Rocky Mountains. Railway line from Winnipeg to Thunder Bay now running. Total length of Canada Pacific completed, about 2,000 miles. Length expected to be completed within one year, from Callander to Port Arthur, 2,500 miles. Government section on Pacific coast, rails already laid, 144 miles. Entire line to Pacific Ocean expected to be running in 1885.

THE GREAT WHEAT BELT

Red River Valley, Saskatchewan Valley, and great Canadian Prairie, the large Wheat Growing Area of the Continent of North America. Richest and Deepest soil, ready for the plough. Heavy Wheat (weighing 65 lb*, to the bushel). Heavy Crops, and Ready Markets. Average product of fair farming, 80 bushels to the acre.

GREAT COAL FIELDS

The Largest Coal Fields in the World, and within easy reach, are in the Canadian North-West, in connection with Iron, Gold, Silver and other valuable minerals.

HOMESTEADS

One hundred and sixty acres given free to every settler in Manitoba and the North-West. Healthy Climate, No Fevers, No Agues, No Endemic Diseases. Full detailed information, in Pamphlets and Maps, furnished (gratis and post free) on application to the

DEPARTMENT OF AGRICULTURE,
OTTAWA, CANADA

14 February

D. L. received a letter from a Joseph Huntley in Canada yesterday. Well, I remember a Joseph Huntley as being one of the laziest workers in the factory some years ago. Surely they could not be the same person. D. L. says that he has just opened a sawmill in a place called Manitoba. D. L. says there is fresh air and free farms there. Joseph Huntley writes that in Manitoba there are no beggars. Free farms and no beggars? What a place Manitoba must be.

31 December

Billy hung up the new year's bag for Wiggins and his crew this morning. Very pretty it was too and stuffed with the sweets we had been up all night making. Martha had painted lots of bright colours on it and tied it with bows and flowers. Well, we all took turns hitting it to make sure it would be good sport for the little children, and Billy got a little carried away. I keep forgetting Dr Watson still has a key, so it was a bit surprising to see him appear at the back door, beneath the bag. He received a rather nasty blow to the nose. He was rather alarmed but saw some humour in it. He asked Martha to call for a doctor before wishing us all a happy new year. Billy made us all laugh when he confessed he didn't know what year came next. A happy new year it shall be.

More celebrities of the time. The 'Hairy Carey' brothers, as they were known, were a feature at the corner of Calder Street and Lynham Road for many years. They sold various items on their stall. These appear, amazingly, to be feet or, rather, an early form of insole. I conjecture that these were not a lucrative line as the benighted souls (?) who had boots could not afford the extra luxury, and those without went barefoot. The woman holding the baby looks equally sceptical. The brothers wore identical beards in homage to their father, whose beard caught fire in a freak accident in a workhouse kitchen when a beef steak virtually exploded. He survived the inferno, but for the rest of his life wore a bag over his head. Tragically, it was whilst wearing the bag that he fell down a manhole. He spent the rest of his life on crutches, but still wore the bag, acquiring the affectionate nickname of 'Sticks Baggy'. Nevertheless, the brothers were always described as endlessly cheerful, but kept away from naked flames – even candles on a birthday cake!

1900

30 June

D. L. delivered today for the weekend. Mr Yarrow must be a very kind gentleman because I always seem to be last on the delivery list. We usually have a good natter, but no time for a chit chat today. Moaner came in the back door and asked whether Mr H. was off chasing Coptic Patriarchs again. I told him I didn't know anything about that but I knew he wouldn't be back for four days. Moaner was about to leave before he announced that Scotland Yard had given him some tickets for a show. D. L. joked that Scotland Yard is a show. Moaner did not laugh, but instead invited me to the Alhambra to see a Hungarian called 'The Handcuff King'.[59]

---

59 Mrs Hudson is obviously referring to the famous escapologist Harry Houdini, who was indeed visiting London at the time. Readers may be interested to note that your humble researcher has history with this particular rascal, having penned a not inconsiderable tome that is still currently available (*Harry Houdini: Man in a Sack*).

He was most excited because they were going to be using his own pair of handcuffs in the show. It's all very exciting and me, at the Alhambra! Time for a new hat.

2 July

Just back from the Alhambra. What a night it was! It was in all the papers. Although, to begin with, I was a little embarrassed that Moaner kept nudging the gentleman next to us to let him know they were his handcuffs. But I think he was most upset at the end when they didn't return them and afterwards he spent most of the time at the stage door demanding them back. He must have another pair. It is nearly midnight as I write this and time to go to bed.

3 July

All is well and the handcuffs have returned. Mr H. came back from his trip this morning and I told him about last night. When I mentioned how the Hungarian gentleman managed to wriggle from Moaner's cuffs, Mr H. became very interested indeed. He wanted to know every single detail of the illusion and I did my best to remember them. Then I told him the gentleman's name and he bolted from his chair, flew down the stairs and out of the front door. Moaner dropped by later in the afternoon and went straight upstairs. A little while later, Mr H. came through the front door and I said that Moaner was waiting in his room. He winked at me and took something out of his pocket. Well, if it wasn't the handcuffs. I went to fetch Moaner as I knew he would be delighted. When we came down, Mr H. was wearing the cuffs.

THE LANDLADY RETURNS 1894–1903

'These are yours, I believe,' he said and, as Moaner went to get his key, Mr H. slipped them off and handed them over. You should've seen the look on Moaner's face.

30 September

D. L. visited this morning. I was surprised when he told me that he was going to Canada after all. I can't say I'm impressed. Silly man. They have wolves over there, don't they? And it's such a big place, I am worried he'll never be heard of again. He jokes that I should come with him but I've never heard such nonsense. There are very few people on God's earth that get my dander up, but he is one. I said that he'd left London once before and come back, so I looked forward to seeing him again in another five years. He laughed and kissed me on the forehead. We can't be having that from a grown man. If he must go – then go! I'll certainly miss the free offal. I can't remember the last time somebody kissed me on the forehead.

4 October

Annie from Mrs Gilbert's has agreed to help out in the kitchen for the time being. Thank heavens, for I am no longer a girl, as Hannah never stops reminding me. Perhaps Annie might be tempted to remain in a more permanent position. Billy would be pleased, as he suggested her in the first place. It even gave me time to sit and read every page of the Family Herald. *A rare treat.*

127

30 November

St Andrew's Day. I read today of the death of Oscar Wilde. I don't know much about plays and things like that as I prefer the music hall, but Billy told me that Wilde once had three plays in London at the same time. Imagine that. What I didn't know was that they removed his name from the posters because of that trial.[60] *Hannah says it was the Marquess of Queensbury that killed him. I don't remember reading about that. One of my lodgers talked about Oscar Wilde a great deal. His name was Mr Dobbes and he used to have even more visitors than Mr H. I remember much laughing going on. He came in one day wearing a ladies hat and asked me if it suited him. I had to say that it didn't. So he gave it to me and we laughed. I think he left the country about five years ago. Not because of the hat, I hope, although I do still wear it.*

---

60 Mrs Hudson is referring to the famous trial of 1895, in which the Marquess of Queensbury (20 July 1844–31 January 1900) successfully defended his reputation in a libel action. The most important thing to note in this case is that the Libel Act of 1843, commonly known as Lord Campbell's Libel Act, enacted several important codifications of and modifications to the common law tort of libel.

J. V. Wilson

Sir Henry Baskerville

Miss V. Hunter

Lord Cantlemere

One of the most interesting of all the pictures here, in my far from humble opinion. These are members of the 'Daughters of the Revolution', wives and widows of American soldiers who were visiting London on a European tour, sponsored by their government.[61] They addressed a rally in Hyde Park, which sadly was rained off after ten minutes. Undaunted, they marched to the Houses of Parliament, where they sang their national anthem and some minstrel ditties. In the centre is Mary Alcott. Could she be related to Louisa May of the same clan and author of *Little Women*, I muse? We may never know. She was apparently a skilled unicyclist and once attempted to pedal across Niagara Falls on a tightrope, but the event was rained off after ten minutes. She was sometimes known as 'unlucky Alcott – the bringer of rain'. The other two women were the formidable Brooklyn Hellcats, who, in suffragette fashion, would chain themselves to railings in a campaign to increase their widows' pensions. Sadly, many papers of the time referred to them, rather scornfully I think, as the 'chain gang'. They did once appear at a function at the White House uninvited. Their hats were their symbol and they would throw them in the air at meetings, which were, hopefully, not rained off after ten minutes!

---

61 The flags contain the correct number of stars for the States of the time. No Hawaii, I fancy!

1901

22 January

God help us – our dear Queen has died. May she rest in peace.

23 January

There has been much talk of the Queen today. Like many people, Mrs Turner was upset when the Queen went to the Isle of Wight after Albert died. In fact, she once said to me that I didn't leave Clerkenwell when I lost Arthur but I don't think that was quite the same thing. Some people were even talking about the Queen and John Brown, but I don't listen to gossip, unless it's family or friends. Mind you, there has been some talk about Mrs Anderson, from down the road, and a plumber. My dear mother used to say live and let live. Mrs B. told a joke about canoodling with a plumber but I'm not writing it down here.

13 February

BEEF TEA

1lb of lean beef, 1 quart of water and 1 spoon of salt.

I have Mr Yarrow trim the fat and bone from the beef usually and for my beef tea I choose the first cut. Slice it into small square pieces and put them into a pan. Add water and put the pan on the fire, before bringing to the boil. Mrs Turner says that you should skim the tea well before cooling but my Arthur used to say that, as in life, the most good usually comes from the scum. Put in the salt when the water boils and simmer for about an hour, then strain. I like to strain my tea through a hair sieve, but Hannah suggests you should take it off your head first to do it. When it is cool, store in the larder with a cloth on top. You'll have to take the fat off and add salt to use it in other cooking.

I was writing down this recipe before making a nice mug of beef tea when I remembered that the late Mr Hudson and I always had beef tea before going to bed. I ought to have some of Arthur's sayings woven into a sampler. He used to say, 'Keep your strength up before tomorrow.' Hannah Brayley says 'Tomorrow is a stranger but today is a friend.' Which is why her washing never gets done.

Once I have finished my tea, I am ready to read a book. I like Wilkie Collins – he helps me sleep. Not that I got much sleep last night, mind. After I'd blown out the candle and settled down, I heard something, a sort of creaking. 'Oh, just the wind,' I thought. But then, my bedroom window, which was ajar, suddenly swung open. I was terrified, I can tell you. I lit the candle and everything seemed alright, but then the door, which I'd also left ajar, opened as well. I jumped out of bed and looked through the door. Someone, or something, was on the landing. I picked up the candle and saw that the coats on the hat stand were moving. Then I heard a very faint sound, like someone laughing. I thought about waking a lodger but then I thought, pull yourself together. It's just the wind, isn't it? I went back to bed but I was still shaking all over. I got up this morning and happened to mention it to Mr H. His eyes lit up. He made me go through the details again and then he examined the door, the landing and the coats with his magnifying glass. Then off he goes to his study and I'm left none the wiser. A few minutes later he calls out and I go up to his room. 'I have exorcised your ghost,' he said. He was sitting in his favourite armchair with a blanket on his lap. He lifted it up. 'Behold, the phantom!' he cried and there was O'Connell, the cat. I was so relieved. Then I remembered the laughing. I'd forgotten to tell Mr H. about that. I don't think I'll ever forget it. I'm watching O'Connell now to see if he laughs again.

22 December

I was visiting Mr Yarrow today to confirm our Christmas order and he told me that he had not received any news from D. L. Hannah was with me and she joked that soon I would be able to shout across the Atlantic with a new machine. Honestly, the things that woman comes out with. Then Mr Yarrow told me that it was true. A Mr Marconi had sent a message across the sea with a thing called a wireless.[62] *How can you do that if there's no wire? Stick to pigeons, I say. They know what they're doing. When Arthur and I were first married, and living in Clerkenwell, there was a pigeon loft next door to us. Mr Tapsell, who kept them, had a reputation as a miser. He was so mean that Arthur used to say that on your birthday, Tapsell would give you a warm handshake and a homing pigeon. Dear Arthur, I think of you always saying 'Coo coo! Coo coo!' like a pigeon every time Mr Tapsell walked past.*

25 December

A very happy Christmas with my tenants. I could tell Mr H. was happy because he kept his paper crown on all day. We spent some of the afternoon playing Fetch the Monkey[63] *and I'll never forget the sight of him, blindfolded with his trouser legs rolled up, trying to hop backwards through the hall. I didn't know both he*

---

62 Mr Marconi's miraculous device was instrumental in saving the lives of several *Titanic* passengers in 1912. Who would've thought that such a noble act would eventually give birth to the iPod? In 1923, Marconi joined the Italian Fascist party and Mussolini made him President of the Royal Academy, proving that such achievements did not go unrewarded.

63 Other popular games of the time included 'Hunt The Chestnut', 'You're The Magistrate', 'Where's Prince Albert?' and 'Squeak, Piggy, Squeak!' This last game has a particular resonance in Philpott family history as when I was a lad (hard to believe, I know!) yours truly was invariably voted Piggy, even by our dear Mamma. It was an accolade that I wore with some pride, year after wonderful year. I would happily volunteer to do so again, if the opportunity ever arose. I wish my brother would remember that it is still a wonderful and important family occasion and that tickets from Thailand are not exactly expensive these days, after all. Merry Christmas, Roger!

and Dr Watson knew all the words to 'Hold Your Hand Out, Naughty Boy'.

Our celebrations were made a little less happy when O'Connell fell asleep by the fire this morning and didn't wake up. Billy has made sure that he is reunited with Mr Disraeli by the coal shed. Peace and goodwill to them both.

1902

4 January

Went to the boxing in Whitechapel with Mrs B. We love it. She says there's nothing she likes more than watching men hit each other. There weren't many women there but she says we're the cream of the cream. So let's have some claret! Sure enough there was some blood, but that's only natural. Josh Makepeace was fighting Bob Worthington and we thought that there's not much peace with Josh around! It went on for quite a long time and when we left they were still at it! We had one or two at the Fox and Hounds and when we got back we had a pretend fight in the kitchen. What anyone would've thought if they came in, I've no idea.

10 January

I was reading the Daily Mail *this morning and, underneath a story about Cecil B. DeMille and Constance Adams, I spied something about Mrs Pankhurst and her daughter Christabel. The paper described them as 'suffragettes'. Although the* Mail mentioned some of their more violent activities, the paper seemed more concerned with the cut of their dresses. I'm not sure what I think of women disrupting meetings, attacking policemen and all that malarkey, but I do admire them. Hannah says Mrs Pankhurst would have been better off marrying a politician and giving him what for and that would have done the trick.

20 May

Wonderful news. Dr Watson told me that Mr Holmes has been offered a knighthood. Well deserved. What will Moaner make of that?

25 May

When Mr H. came in today, I congratulated him on his knighthood and did a little curtsey. He smiled and then informed me that he had declined the honour. I happen to think he's rather bold but can't help thinking he might've taken it from the old Queen.

2 June

Moaner popped in. Mr H. was out but, whilst he waited, he offered to help me mend my larder hinges. Quite agitated he was, like a man with a mouse in his shoes. He couldn't stand still whilst we re-hung the door and I very nearly dropped it on his big toe as he danced around. So I sat him down and asked him what the matter was. Moaner's only just heard about Mr H. and the knighthood. I didn't have the heart to tell him that Mr H. is turning it down. Moaner did not stay long after that – muttered something about 'His Holiness' and left. I don't think retirement will suit him.

6 July

To: Mrs Sarah Hudson
221b Baker Street
London, W.
England

Dear Nanny,

I hope to write you many such letters, but work here is going so well that I worry I will not be given the time. The beds are comfortable, the food is plentiful and the land is vast. Haunting but beautiful. I feared my back would not be able to take the hours of bending and sifting required finding these precious nuggets, but I think the fresh air and friends have strengthened it!

When we are able to feast on some meat (usually caribou), I think of how I would set aside the best cut for you. I never told Mr Yarrow, but that brisket you were able to serve your tenants the night before I left was meant for Mrs Turner! I thought you'd find that funny, tho' now that I write this, I do feel a pang of regret and feel like I should send her some trinket by way of recompense.

We are being taken into the local town tonight as a reward for our hard labours. We have been told that we will meet some townsfolk and even hear some music.

I will write again when I have more time.

Ever your friend,

D. L.

21 July

Dr Watson moved his belongings out today. To Queen Anne St of all places. A great many doctors there to keep him and his new wife company, no doubt. Though you wouldn't know it, he'd barely been gone two days when he was back here, scribbling away after Mr H.'s every move. Poor Mrs Watson.

1903

5 July

Quite the most delightful day today. I thought I would take a stroll with my new parasol. Much to my distress, however, it is missing from the cupboard. I've a good mind to set Mr H. on the case, but he is nowhere to be found.

9 July

There was a Chinese sailor[64] *poking around in the alley this morning looking at fish heads in the gutter. He was squatting there, transfixed, for many minutes. I couldn't help going over to look myself. I asked him what he was doing and he replied, in perfect*

---

64 London's first Chinatown was established in Limehouse in the 1890s when Chinese sailors were stranded by the Blue Funnel Line. The BFL offered them no return ticket to China. They settled around Limehouse Causeway, hence the names Canton Street and Pekin Street. One wonders whether Kensal Rise was once Kensal Rice. Perhaps Basingstoke may one day become Beijingstoke! Little joke there, readers, allow me that.

To: Mrs Sarah Hudson
221b Baker Street
London, W.
England

Dear Nanny,

Just a short line to let you know how thing are here in Manitoba. We are going on fairly well but of course we wish things were a bit better with the weather. It is so cold here but I would welcome some rain. I'm saying so 'cos of my crops and my cattle but on the whole I'm very happy here. You were right. There are wolves and they do danger us, but I can put your mind at rest by saying they are not after me – only our cows. The boys here are teaching me well and the town is growing so much. Well Nanny, I believe I made a little mistake in the last letter by putting in the name of Clara when mentioning my time at church. She is indeed a cousin and helping me with the farm, but she is also now my wife. I always thought St Saviours in Bow would see yours truly dressed in a Topper, but it appears that moment has been saved for St Hilda's in Moose Jaw instead. I must go now. I hope the meat is still arriving!

Hoping to hear from you soon.

Kind remembrance to one and all at home.

From your friend,

D. L.

English, 'Making a study of the gutting practices of Baker Street landladies, Mrs Hudson.' 'When will you be pleased to dine, Mr Holmes?' I said. 'Seven-thirty the day after tomorrow.' I don't think I'll ever get used to his nonsense.

10 July

Since we've lost the doctor, I have more and more to depend on Billy to help me out with things. He's ever so big now, is Billy. Quite a shock some days to think of that little ten-year-old quivering in D. L.'s coat. Well, he caught this ragged old man trying to steal up the stairs at lunchtime, his pockets full of rags and string. I need not have worried. It was Mr H. again and still he wants no dinner.

11 July

Mystery solved. Another fine day and I decided to venture outside to collect some ingredients for the supper. Imagine my surprise when I spied this old lady twirling about in the park with my missing parasol. I decided to follow her and see what she was up to. I was so convinced that it was Mrs Turner and was about to caution her when she turned around, took the pipe from her mouth and winked at me. I am getting too old for this.

Later on, when I went upstairs to ask for my parasol, I was met with a very unhelpful silence. He didn't turn round and I left, assuming he was in one of his moods. Then I saw Mr H. and Billy coming towards me. I'd been looking at the dummy! So long as he doesn't want me to wheel it from one side of the room to the other, I don't mind. Let that be Billy's privilege.

Well, I don't know if I'm allowed to write this, but we had the

Prime Minister, the Home Secretary and Lord Cantlemere with us this afternoon.

I am very proud of Annie today who was able to cook a delightful plate for them all at such very short notice. She will make a very fine cook one day and I am ever grateful to her for all that she is doing. Her friend, Charlotte Honeychurch, who used to work in the royal kitchens, often sends her letters from Windsor containing recipes. We were very grateful for this Aylesbury duck suggestion as I know it to be one of the Home Secretary's favourites.

ROAST AYLESBURY DUCK

Mr Yarrow had dressed the ducks well and he'd hung them for two days, just as I like them. My mother used to say that cooks should wait until the flies come, but I think that a little too much. I made a stuffing of sage and onion for the ducks and Annie basted them whilst I was attempting to retrieve my parasol. When I returned, I took them to the kitchen table and sprinkled them lightly with flour before returning them to the fire. Once the steam had risen, after about half an hour, I took them to Mr H.'s rooms, with lots of gravy poured around the side of the plate. I made some Cumberland sauce for it, as I know how much the doctor likes it. Every cook should know this good sauce. Boil down strips of well-cut orange and lemon peel in one pan, and redcurrant jelly and port in another. Mix well mustard and ginger with lemon juice, orange juice, the port, redcurrant and the strips of lemon and orange. Mrs Beeton recommends green peas with the duck but Charlotte suggests that we use beets. Well I never. There were such compliments. Even from Lord Cantlemere. I had heard that he was a bit stern, but he made a special point of commending Annie on her cooking. Mr H. doesn't like him at all. I cannot understand why.

12 July

Billy tells me that he and Annie plan to marry. I am so happy for them and I already have a wedding gift in mind. I must do my best to keep it a secret until that day.

Billy also told me that Lord Cantlemere had something to do with the theft of that jewel. What an unspeakable prig!

9 October

Mr H. received some news today that caused him much distress. Billy took him a note and when he read it, his face fell. There were then strict instructions not to disturb him for the rest of the day. This is not the first time he has demanded this, but somehow today seemed different. Billy told me that the note had the name of Adler on it. I told him off for reading a tenant's correspondence but then remembered that it must be to do with that opera singer who died last week in New York. She visited here some twenty years ago and Mr H. still mentions her from time to time. I think there must be more to this than I would care to ask him. Perhaps the doctor can help.

24 November

Mr H. gave me his notice today. Very sad, I was, especially when Martha reminded me it'd been twenty-two years since he and the doctor first moved in. Not without their moments I will say and there are things I won't miss – bullet holes for one thing. Where am I going to find someone who'll pay me such a handsome rent? Mr H. assures me that won't be a problem. If I didn't know any better, and I rarely do with him, I'd think he was up to something again. I asked him if he was planning to go gallivanting off to Switzerland or up a mountain and leave me half in a tizzy over his wellbeing. But no. He's off to Sussex where he's bought a farm. You can never tell with him. Mr H. the farmer? He told me that he was going to watch bees. I told him he could watch bees here in London. Why did he need to go all the way to Sussex to watch bees? Still, he's always known his own mind, that one, and there's no sense in arguing as he'll bark something stern at you and dash off to his rooms.

18 December

Billy told me today about two brothers in America called Orville and Wilbur who flew in a machine at a place called Kitty Hawk. Billy says the machine was called 'heavier than air', so it's hard to believe they flew. It's difficult enough getting a piano off the ground and I can't imagine something that big. I can't keep up with everything these days. Nothing in America surprises me. I wonder if D. L. has heard about it?

20 December

That's it. He's gone. And with nothing resembling a farewell. No sign of a note or any such thing. Just some men who came to take his belongings away – a few boxes and a portmanteau.

21 December

Very surprised when Wiggins knocked on my door first thing this morning with a package. Happy to see the boy is now quite the man. You'll never guess what was inside. A jar of Sussex honey, only there was no honey in it! Inside, Mr H. had left me two years' worth of rent, the key to his desk and an invitation to visit him. He always liked the dramatic. A trip to the seaside is most welcome and I'm sure there'll be honey there. I like honey.

23 December

After carol singing at the Brayleys, Hannah introduced me to a gentleman in a bright green suit from Enmore Park who was visiting her. Hannah jokes that he was Father Christmas taking a much needed rest. I think he is related to her in some way but I am not sure how. Quite a gruff fellow, but he asked me about my rooms and, for some reason, I told him that we had nothing available. Hannah quickly reminded me about my first floor. I suppose I have become so used to Mr H. being at 221b, I had all but forgotten.

These children appear to have been playing 'Maypole Lamp',[65] a popular street game of the time. However, it was not popular with parents due to the instability of gas lamps, which caused several accidents (see below). One of the children would wield what was known as a 'wiggle stick' with which children would poke passers-by and should the person react with violence, the other children would then have to retreat to the nearest lamppost. This caused mayhem on the streets of London. The graffiti, on the doors behind, is indecipherable but may refer to some contemporary political event (or similar). It is interesting to note that the boys by the doors are all wearing caps thought to prevent cholera. The woman positioned at the back on the left, presumably the mother of one or more of the children in front of her, is seen in another photo of the time holding the 'firm' rope, a cautionary measure, as a gas lamp once fell down in Southwark, killing a cat and causing a horse to stampede, overturning a hansom cab in the process.

I've been unable to ascertain the exact street depicted but think it may well be in Pimlico.

---

65 'Maypole Lamp' (the song) was sung on occasion by Bella Lomax and gave rise to a dance called 'The Maypole Polka', which had a brief vogue.

IV

Life after Holmes
1904–11

1904

6 January

Hannah's friend, who I now know is a professor, has finally moved in. Such a funny beard. He's rather a large man and I must say that he has quite a large head. If it weren't for his clothes, I would say that Bruin the bear had become my new lodger! Certainly the bellowing, roaring and rumbling make it feel like there is a wild animal upstairs. Certainly if O'Connell were still here he'd have something to say! Billy is a little unsure of him, but then I think that is because he could fit Billy in his top hat. If the professor is half as interesting as the last tenants, I will be delighted. I never thought I would write such a thing. Mr H. and the doctor will certainly be difficult to follow, but I have a feeling that our new lodger will offer some interesting stories as well. He informs me that although he intends to make this his home, he will likely spend most of the year in South America. So long as his rent is here, he can go wherever he likes.

12 June

I finally went down to see Mr Holmes in Sussex. I've been post-poning it, as I didn't know what to expect and I thought I might be upset. How wrong I was. It was a lovely sunny day and I took a pony and trap from the station. One curious thing, though. I found it strange that the driver didn't know who Mr Holmes was. I thought everyone did. When I got to the villa, I saw him wearing his beekeeper's hat in the middle of some hives. I called out his name and he turned round. It was so good to see him again. He took the hat off, came over and shook my hand. We went inside and there was Martha looking very contented. She handed me a pair of fancy mittens that she had knitted for me and I have to say I was very touched. She said that she'd always thought my gloves were not warm enough for London in winter and she is right. Such a lovely gift. I have missed her. Mr H. then said that he would make us tea for a change, not the other way round. If it hadn't been for the sunshine and all the lovely trees around us, I might have thought we were back in Baker Street. I'd never seen Mr H. like that before. He was so calm and he smiled often. He also asked after Billy and wanted to be told about life at 221b. I told him about the professor and he seemed to know rather a lot about him, saying that I am very lucky to have such a distinguished scientist under my roof. What he doesn't know about the evolution of the vertebrae is not worth knowing, Mr H. told me. I thought of complimenting Mr H. on his own scientific achievements but thought he'd had enough compliments for one day. Then I noticed that he hadn't mentioned Dr Watson, but when I did – well, he talked and talked, making me think that although he'd found a new life he still missed the old one. As I was leaving, he told me about a dance that he'd noticed bees do to tell each other where the good flowers are. And do you know? He did it for me as I waved goodbye to them both. I chuckled all the way to the station. I got home with a warm feeling and a little sadness. I'm happy for him now but the hurly burly of his time here is missing. Water under the bridge, as Hannah says, but I still like to stand on that bridge from time to time. And I have two jars of honey.

1906

10 March

The Baker Street and Waterloo Railway opened today. Billy went but I didn't. Instead I sat in the kitchen and watched the crockery rattle. It was either the Railway, or Prof. C. is assaulting another member of the press upstairs.

26 June

A Mr Sessions from the Daily Mail *visited the professor today. I don't think he even made it into the room before Prof. C. went for him and threw him down the stairs. I thought Mr H. was the very worst tenant in London. I think we have a challenger.*

24 November

Billy and Annie were married today. If I had a son, I could not have wanted a more perfect day for his wedding. Bright sun and the most colourful flowers. Annie wore her mother's veil and looked pretty as a picture. I half expected Mr H. and the doctor to turn up but it was not to be.

D. L. sent a telegram to celebrate the nuptials and I finally gave them their gift. Their copy of the lease for 221b.

POST OFFICE TELEGRAM

Received at:

Oxford Street Exchange, 23 November

Congratulations William and Ann. Always said you two would make a good match. Like me and Clara. Wait till you meet your new cousin! There is always a nest here for you lovebirds. Write soon. Uncle D. L., Manitoba

Parson Nicholas

Dr A. C. Smith

Dr J. Mortimer

LADY CARRINGTON

Another street scene. The woman in the centre is holding her baby as well as some washing that she would've taken in from one of her clients. This was a common practice among the working classes, alleviating their poverty.[66] The man on the right is smiling, maybe at the sight of the woman on the left or perhaps at some private thought he is currently entertaining. The child is wearing the obligatory scarf – infant mortality due to hypothermia was rife at the time. As to the woman on the left, she appears to looking at something out of the picture. So with the best will in the world, I cannot help you there. Please notch it up as one of my few failures. If you'd be so kind! On the top of the picture there appears to be a security camera, but I think we can dismiss that supposition for obvious reasons.[67]

---

66 'Washington' – a place name that derived from 'Washing' and 'Tun', the latter being a barrel in which washing was kept. Other synonyms being 'Cask' and 'Firkin' (not much used these days due to misunderstandings!).

67 The bucket has no handle – limiting its practicality one would think.

1907

23 January

I ventured to the Holborn Empire today. I tend to go out most days, now that Billy and Annie can take care of things. My rooms are not what they were since Mr H. and the doctor moved out. It is Hannah's birthday next month and she is such a fan of Mr George Robey that I thought I would buy some tickets. Well, I had got no further than Oxford Street when a woman I recognised from the Tivoli (she knew the Two Bobs when there was only one of them) thrust a leaflet into my hand.

HOLBORN EMPIRE

HIGH HOLBORN, W.C.
Manager CLAUDE E. MARNER
Twice Nightly at 6.15 & 9.10
MATINEES, THURSDAY & SATURDAY AT 2.30
AN APPEAL FOR JUSTICE

I feel it my duty to place before my numerous Patrons a few facts in connection with the Music Hall Strike, feeling that by adopting such a course, my position will be justified in the eyes of the Public.

By virtue of Agreement between myself and the Variety Artistes Federation, made in December last, I agreed to accept the undermentioned conditions and terms made by them, and these terms I have loyally adhered to.

1. I agree to pay all Musicians and Stage hands in my employ at the Halls under my control, the full TRADE UNION rate of wages, and to pay, pro rata, for all extra performances, including Matinees.

2. To show no bias or prejudice against any Artists or Musician – who was, or might in future, become Member of the National Alliance of Artistes, Musicians and Stage employees.

3. To pay additional wages to all Stage Hands at a rate which was mutually agreed between the Alliance and myself.

4. To refer to a Board of Arbitration, consisting of Two Nominees appointed by myself, Two Nominees appointed by the Alliance, and an independent Chairman, all disputes which might thereby arise. The Agreement has been strictly adhered to by me in every way.

A little further down the street, I was given another leaflet.

Music Hall War

Mr GIBBONS – ANOTHER UNTRUTH

Mr Gibbons says he has paid and is paying, the Trade Union Rate asked for by the National Association of Theatrical (Stage) Employees.

THIS STATEMENT IS UNTRUE

Mr Gibbons, prior to the agreement with the Alliance, paid less than 21/4d per hour to some of the staff, others were paid 11s per week less than the Union rate on the Evening of the Saturday last, after Mr Gibbons had again repeated it, and broken his word of honour.

SUPPORT THE ARTISTS AND WORKERS IN THEIR STRUGGLE FOR FAIR TERMS AND CONDITIONS.

Published by the Co-operative Printing Society Ltd. Tudor St EC and published by J. B. Williams, 9 Great Newport St, WC.

Well, I didn't even know there was a strike. What is the world coming to? Mr Gibbons' shows are always such a jolly affair, it's a shame to see them stopped in this way. I wonder if Bella Lomax has joined the picket line? They'd certainly not get through.

24 January

Hannah told me all about the strike. Mrs Turner's daughter sometimes works at the Tivoli and apparently when Mr Gibbons asked Little Tich to defy the strike, he said that he was too busy learning a new cornet solo and could not tear himself away. Miss Turner then told Hannah that Marie Lloyd's advice was to send for Wagstaff and Williams: The Yodelling Vicars. She said they could empty any theatre. Hannah saw them at Hawkins' Music Hall once and said an old woman was trampled in the rush for the exits.

1910

7 May

As I sat at breakfast today, Martha brought me in the Morning
Post. *Lined with black, the inside pages revealed the King
was dead.*

*I can remember only ever twice before having had such a shock.
The day they told me about you, Arthur, and the day Mr Mycroft
Holmes told me about Mr H. disappearing.*

*Martha told me that the King only had a bronchitis attack the
day before. How quickly these things happen. It made me think of
Hannah, who is not very well at the moment and who I must visit
in the morning.*

8 May

*Almost everyone I see is dressed in black today, just as it was for the
Queen's funeral. We thought she was going to live forever and now
the King has left us too. I do believe he did some good, though, and
was a tonic for the nation. If he did some of the things that people*

*say he did, well, that's none of our business. He made us all smile
and that is the important thing.*

17 May

*The King is now in Westminster Hall. When I visited Hannah today,
I told her that Lillie Langtry and Sarah Bernhardt might be at the
funeral and wondered what Queen Alexandra might think. Hannah
said that Alexandra was probably just delighted to know where her
husband was for a change. I think Hannah must be feeling better.*

19 May

*Billy and Annie returned from Westminster Hall this afternoon. I
could not believe how long they had been away, but Billy told me
half the world was there. Annie said that the other half will be at
the funeral tomorrow. The coffin had beautiful wreaths on it but
Annie was most excited by the crown, the garter, the orb and the
sceptre that sat on top. They say it was hard work and the nation's
burden that killed him. Hannah said it was something else that
killed him yesterday and I don't mind how well she is feeling, there
is no call for that.*

20 May

*I felt strong enough to join Billy, Annie and Martha in honouring
our King today. What a spectacle it was. London was filled with
hundreds of people who had been waiting since it was dark to
get their place on the street. By the time we had taken a position
near Whitehall, it was near ten o'clock and the procession was
nearly with us. I was able to see the coffin with eight horses in*

front, covered with a Union Jack and the crown and regalia that Billy and Annie mentioned. This was followed by the King's horse with nobody riding – just his boots in the stirrups. I thought this rather sad until the King's little dog Caesar came along, led by a Highlander. I do not care much for dogs, but there was this little thing frisking and yapping at the crowd so much that Billy and I began to laugh at the silliness of it all. Then came King George, the Kaiser, the Duke of Connaught and seven other Kings that I did not know the names of.[68] Martha thought that the Kaiser looked rather pompous as the crowd cheered Caesar, with Billy joking that they must have got their names mixed up in the processional order. As we walked home, I could not help spare a thought for dear old Queen Alexandra who had to sit in her coach and watch it all, one slow step at a time.

---

68 The procession did in fact include Kaiser Wilhelm II, Emperor of Germany, who barely a decade later was disgraced and living in exile in Holland, and George I, King of the Hellenes, who was assassinated in 1913 by a drunken vagrant whilst walking in Thessaloniki. His son, Constantine, Duke of Sparta, was also at the funeral and succeeded George, but was exiled twice before dying prematurely. It is interesting to note here that Constantine's successor, Alexander, died in 1920 after monkeys attacked his dog and, while defending his animal, he received a bite that turned to septicaemia. Archduke Franz Ferdinand of Austria was there – as any schoolboy or schoolgirl (even these days) might be able to tell you, he was assassinated in 1914, an incident that occurred in the proverbial powder keg that was the Balkans of the time and directly contributed to the start of the First World War. This, of course, was a conflict that accounted for the deaths of nearly 9 million people. Prince Michael Romanov was also at Edward VII's funeral, and he would be murdered along with his family at the hands of the Bolsheviks during the Russian Revolution. Albert, King of Belgium, Alfonso, King of Spain, and Manuel, King of Portugal along with the aforementioned Constantine were all exiled. Ferdinand, King of Bulgaria merely abdicated.

Eureka! This is Hannah Brayley in an uncharacteristically serious pose (or do we detect the hint of a playful smile?) at the door of her residence. With her skittish behaviour, she seemed to act as a catalyst for Mrs Hudson – a practising catalyst you might say! The echoes of the laughter she provoked resound through the years. Mrs Brayley subsequently lost a leg in an accident but, undeterred, regaled customers with her impression of the newly infamous Long John Silver, complete with crutch and parrot. I venture to think that she was the Ann Widdecombe of her day!

And with our final picture I bid adieu to you dear reader, and embark upon the next exciting leg of the Philpott adventure, where my motto is – wherever the wind may take you, just float along and enjoy the view.

Oliver Philpott
Crawley, 2011

NOTE

This book is now dedicated to our researcher, Oliver Philpott, who, after completing his duties was reported missing. Details of his disappearance are unclear, though it is believed that in the course of researching *The Effect of the Eighteenth-Century Whaling Industry on the Development of the Corset 1707–1821*, his work took him to the Arctic. His empty kayak was last seen drifting among ice floes off Greenland.

'Oliver Philpott? A constant visitor.'
Sir Hadlee Caincross, Chairman of the National Archives, Kew.

Oliver Philpott 1963–2012

V

The east wind comes 1912—14

1912

17 September

Martha received a letter today from Mr H., no less. I cannot quite believe it but she tells me a position has become available with a Mr Von Bork in Harwich and that Mr H. has personally put her name forward. How did he know that we had an elderly aunt who lived in the town?

I had not for one minute expected Martha to do anything other than stay at 221b for the rest of her days, but it seems she is going to meet Mr H. at Claridge's to discuss the post.

I do wish he would visit.

19 September

Martha has been my maid here from the very beginning, so a very important person is leaving us. I am rather upset with Mr Holmes, I have to say, but I suppose every bird must fly one day.

The strange thing is that ever since seeing the Kaiser at the King's funeral, she's thought all Germans to be rummy old coves. I hope he will pay her more than I did.

1914

30 July

Billy and Annie signed the lease this morning and we had some-thing of a party to celebrate our exchange. I feel very sure that 221b is now in good hands. Much leg twisting in the kitchen and I had to lie down for the remainder of the day.

31 July

A fearful headache this morning. It felt best if I gained some air to clear my thoughts. Besides, Billy and Annie will want to get started on their new life without me cluttering their feet. I took the omnibus to the Strand and decided to take a walk along the Thames. I would have ventured to Clerkenwell but I fear yesterday has quite tired me out. So I sat on a bench in Victoria Embankment Gardens and watched a Linley brick barge float by. On its way to Bermondsey no doubt. Where it all began for me. Where it all began for you, too, Arthur. It might even have been the same barge that you used to collect lime from; in fact, I'm certain of it. You felt sure that one day you would own that company. Perhaps you might have done, my sweet. You seemed so confident in everything that was to come for us and you used to say that anything was possible here. How sad you would be now to see London as it is. I do not like that you didn't get to share in all the adventures in Baker Street, my dear Arthur, with Mr H. and the doctor. I have a feeling that you might have thought them both entertaining. How they have helped this country in ways that we will never know. I look at the soldiers in the park and I realise that we may need them now more than ever. I looked at London today and wondered if it will be the same again.

This is the first time I have written my diary away from my kitchen. I don't know why but I did not think I wanted to write this evening. I want to finish my polishing, sit in the corner of the kitchen and watch the embers fade.

The sun is shining and now the rain has finished, the air smells sweeter. The walk back to Baker Street is always pleasant.

Goodnight Arthur, my dearest, wherever you are.

Index

Also available from The Robson Press

ERIC MORECAMBE:
LOST AND FOUND

EDITED BY GARY MORECAMBE

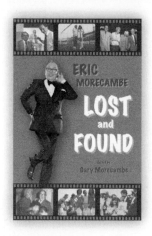

As one half of Morecambe & Wise, Eric Morecambe occupied
a special place in the nation's affections. Twenty-eight years after
his death, the country still mourns and misses 'the one with the
glasses'. Now, a wealth of newly discovered photos from dusty
archives across the UK show this much-cherished comedy maestro
at home and at work, in intimate family portraits and with comedy
heroes from Tommy Cooper to Ronnie Barker.

*"Eric drew us in. He could say and do very little and we would laugh. So,
even now, when we know what's coming, we have a childish excitement just to
be in the room with him again. His work doesn't tire."* Miranda Hart

240pp hardback, £18.99
Available now in all good bookshops or order from
www.therobsonpress.com